THE TROUBLE WITH NOUNS

A STORY BY NICOLE WHITE

Cover art by MarleeMade

The Trouble with Nouns
A story by Nicole White
www.thetroublewithnouns.com

ISBN: 978-0-646-97475-0

THE TROUBLE WITH NOUNS

A STORY BY NICOLE WHITE

Part One

A PRISONER IN AN UNLOCKED HOUSE

HINDSIGHT

It's hard to tell whether it was his theory or the sleep lab which did the most damage. Looking back it's safe to say they each fed into the other, compounding the issues at hand like a jackhammer, but since his theory was an ambush, and the experiment more in the arena of voluntary, I feel no qualms about making him the scapegoat. Of course, it's easy to condemn him at this hour, especially since he's not here and there's no-one else around to blame, just this one bird calling dawn, echoing his words and embedding the seed even further. But that's the trouble with hindsight—the more frequent the visit, the more pervasive the discord.

See, he—Thermos Man—usually sits alone. From mid-morning to lunch on most weekdays he occupies the right side of a park bench visible from my bedroom window, adjacent to the school gates, about fifty steps into the park. His manner lends a certain amount of predictability, the way he smiles *hello* and nods *good day* to passers-by, watching birds, mostly with contentment, but with occasional traces of regret crossing his forehead. Regret is an easy one to recognise, especially in an older person; it's all to do with the depth and direction of their wrinkles and the shape of their brows. It's not impossible to recognise on a younger individual, the indicators are just more fleeting and less ingrained.

Before the encounter, I considered Thermos Man pleasant and non-threatening. His predictablility lending a level of comfort hard to come by in my daily encounters, until one day, about eight months ago, when he took me by surprise insisting I join him in sampling some of his homemade iced tea. It's not something I would usually do, accept an invitation like that, but since I had no other pressing engagements to tend to, on this day, I accepted his offer.

"Shhh," he hushed as I sat, silently. "Hear that?"

"Hear what? The cars?"

"No."

"The kids?"

"No love, the birds."

"Oh."

While he fills a cup, he goes on to tell me his theory, which suggests that the birds can tell when a person is in mourning, so they sing songs in this specific key, a decibel that travels directly to this certain part of the brain which expands into the stress of loss so it doesn't feel so bad. I must admit, it sounded great at the time, something of a nice coping mechanism, but that was then and this is now, and now I wish I could erase the correlation because I no longer hear any melody to their calls, all I hear are their specific conversation points.

The patterns began to emerge after a few weeks of attention and with a minor effort on my part, it all began to make perfect sense. I think they know that I know, the birds, and now they're messing with me. They know I know at least half of what they're on about, so now they dish it out one bead at a time as if something terrible might happen if they divulged all their secrets at once.

It goes something like this:

Monday mornings are slow, spacious and layered with instruction. The seasoned ones start with cautions about what to expect from sub-streetlight landings, warnings about phantom clouds that look like real clouds, and best practices on how to avoid high impact neck compression. These reminders go on repeat until a spritely one starts up like he's allocating teams and districts, which is news that always riles the young ones who chime in overtop, restless with the stationary nature of the meetings. I understand their impatience completely, but also acknowledge the necessity of clarifying the daily plan early, since the up-start of city racket will soon impede any chance of a long distance broadcast.

Flight paths are lazy on Mondays; movements have less to do with inspired missions and more to do with obligation.

Weekdays around three their calls sound deranged. The medley tells of trouble, probably because the kids have been set free and there's lunacy in the way they run from the school gates.

Fridays and Saturdays around six the mood's a bit lighter, though still manic, as they congregate atop the new season foliage to recount the day's events all at once. This usually generates a static, but by this time I've got too much pool water in my ears to translate any details.

Sometimes, in the night hours, a wise crone will sing her song to me, baiting me to calibrate to her language. It's just me and her and I can tell by her tone that she knows me, repeating the call like she does, but every time it feels like we're getting somewhere, there's a sudden outburst two streets over from an insomniac pair who've likely just witnessed a crime, so I lose my place and all progress is lost.

Being a Tuesday and pre-dawn not a lot is happening on the bird front. It's not the hour to transmit secrets so they're mostly relaxed, enjoying the last remnants of civilian unconsciousness. I might've been in a position to enjoy the moment too, had I not woken perched on the ten metre diving platform above the community pool with a teen lifeguard on opening duties below.

This situation is not ideal, but I'm close to home, and so far, undetected.

I roll to the edge and watch this kid, impressed by his work ethic at such an early hour. He's methodical and accurate in his efforts, no movement superfluous.

He's hosing down sun-chairs, checking the meters, dragging the lane ropes out one stream at a time. Fishing out wayward foliage, stray chip packets, and somehow he manages to cover the diving pool with a blue tarp effortlessly, which really seems like a job better suited for two. Had the likelihood my intervention wouldn't lead to incrimination, I might've got down to help him.

With four sun-chairs left to upturn, his behaviour veers on the edge of suspicious. He's at the halfway mark determining wind direction, when he turns one-eighty and bolts down the length of the pool, stopping at this blue man-hole cover where he kneels, removes the cover and goes in shoulder deep to retrieve a jar. From the jar comes a small zip-lock bag and from that he extracts half a joint and a lighter.

Moments later a flume of smoke floats in the direction of the community gardens which is when the office door swings open and smacks into the brickwork. Concrete dust sprinkles from the wall and this bald guy limps out. He's got a sweat-stained singlet stretching over his beach-ball gut and his intense squint concentrates centrally like he's been looking at something small and far away most days of his life.

In an effort to block out the rising sun, his left arm goes up like he's hailing Hitler and the kid is stuck frozen with his arms stiff by his sides like he's holding two invisible bags of cement. Meanwhile, I'm stunted, emphatically hoping this old guy is temporarily blinded so the kid isn't busted, and double hoping neither of them notice me on the diving platform watching all this unfold from prayer position.

With every step he takes, Limp-gut throws out another demand.

"It's ten-to-six. Why ya standin' there?

Those other lane-ropes need to go out.

There's shit in the third cubicle in the men's.

And check those meters too.

Useless twerp."

Like his ambitions for the kid, Limp-gut's feet get ahead of him and he stumbles forward about a metre which infuriates him so much it looks like he might snap a tibia purely from rage tremors. He deems further exertion not worth the effort and when the door meets the brickwork again, I knew we were safe.

Seven samaritans later, when the kid is filling a bucket, I jump.

Neil continues adjusting his goggles.

Kid takes the bucket into the men's.

No-one saw a thing.

SUBVERT (PULP)

Halfway across Lincoln, a swarm of navy-clad kids less than half the fence height come running to me like I'm a magnet and they too, are magnets. For about two steps I think it's because they've recognized my efforts in heresy and wish to celebrate with me, but gratification quickly deflates when I realise the true cause of their enthusiasm.

"Could ya get our ball for us please miss? It's over there going under that brown car. See?"

The request comes from a freckly-faced boy of about eight, or a small twelve. He speaks in a pitch that sounds like he's been wound up by a key in his back. This ignites nostalgia for vanilla ice-cream from a cone, and makes me infinitely thankful I'm on this side of the fence.

Little fingers point through the chain link in the direction of a green ball rolling toward the two-toned brown and beige car that hasn't moved in at least two years and probably couldn't even if someone tried. Next to the car is a teacher talking to a dad who's holding a little girl all dressed up for a ball. She's too young for school and too hot to care. The ball rolls from the pavement to the gutter and she doesn't do a thing about it.

Ice-cream kid mirrors me on his side of the fence, dancing on tiptoes under his navy broad-brimmed hat about three years too big for him. He's about to walk straight passed yesterday's word, soggy from last night's tropical downpour, and very likely, completely unsalvageable.

"Hey, what's that?" I slow my pace, eyes set on the note.

"What's what?" His voice pitches again. He's looking around the paper and beyond the paper but misses it entirely. I point to it.

"That—there in the fence. It's some sort of note or something."

He engages zoom, leaps in, extracts the note and tries to unfold it, but it breaks apart in his fingers.

Pulp.

He looks up at me with eyes wide and green, seeking an explanation.

"It's all wet."

"Can you read it?"

"No. It's all blurry."

A few bitumen dents in my knees later, I launch the ball into the yard. The kid drops the pulp, runs in a circle and calculates its descent perfectly so it lands in his waiting arms. Slightly disorientated, he runs back to his friends, skimming the skirt of the yard duty teacher who's eating what looks to be a curried egg sandwich. She's got her eyes to the sky too, until she steps over the soggy note which seems to alert all her senses. She looks me dead in the eye like someone whispered in her ear—*that's her.*

—◇—

Fortunately neither Zac nor Gustave's caretaker notice me as I dart across the road. They're at the foot of the stairs talking about bills or the council, I imagine, so I take the back-alley with the hope that the extended route will buy me enough time to think of an explanation for my saturation.

When I turn into the alley I'm faced with an oven angled like it's challenging me to a duel. The initial shock soon wears off when I deduce people often upgrade ovens for an assortment of practical and economic reasons and it's then I discover it's The Dope Haus residents who are dealing with the upgrade. At least a party of three.

"Sorry guys, I really thought it would fill the hole."

Not Eyebrows.

"You tried, but maybe measure it next time."

Definitely Eyebrows.

"You guys—you're not even listening to me." Definitely not Eyebrows. "She has this totally other life. The whole time, I never wondered. I never wondered what she did and now look where I am."

"You're in exactly the same position you've always been in."

"But I'm not—don't you see?"

Although I'm well aware they've probably sensed my presence and are likely attuned to the fact that this isn't my floor, I still feign difficulty with the latch so I can hear more.

"Consider yourself lucky Clive. Lucky she didn't catch on."

"Lucky? Lucky to be alone? Lucky to have been deceived for so long?"

Clive's questions elicit a dense sigh as if the conversation point wore out long ago.

"It doesn't sound like she deceived you man, it sounds like it just meant more to you than it did to her. Now, who wants to do fifteen push-ups with me to get psyched?"

No-one says anything about the push-ups, the love dilemma or the oven the whole way up the fire escape. On the last spiral turn I notice they haven't made any progress on their fort, nor had I on my excuse.

Zac appears beyond my reflection. He's in the kitchen doorway with this look about him that says—*I'm on a mission: steer the-fuck clear.*

Handlebar shoulders engage as I enter.

"Didn't you hear me knocking?"

"No, I just got home. This is me, getting home."

Zac's moist too, but from sweat, not pool water. It turns the first few inches of his hair a dark mousy brown instead of mousy brown. Helmet marks indent the rest of it.

"Why are you all wet?"

"I went for a swim."

"In all your clothes?"

He pauses the removal of his backpack for an answer he already knew.

"Yes."

His usual eyebrow dance of disapproval ensues, but the lethargy that follows the twenty five stair climb in chlorine soaked clothes prevents me from clinging to the annoyance. It's a small feat, but I relish in it anyway while I fill a glass with water. Pipes bang and rattle to life and the leak streams consistent. I turn the tap off gently so I don't make it worse.

Zac removes some textbooks from his bag, followed by his purple lunchbox and an overlooked blackened banana—the discovery of which does not help alleiviate his frown.

"So it's probably a long shot, but you're not going anywhere near Uscray today are you?" He pulls out a yellow envelope marked with a name and address, smeared in parts with spots of wet—likely banana juice.

I shake my head.

"Does it have something to do with that envelope?"

He nods.

"Selby asked me to deliver it for her and I just went to meet the guy but he never showed up. Turns out there was a miscommunication where she said library at Uscray but I thought she meant library at Hudson—since that's where she goes to school and all. Anyway, now there's a redirect but my mother just called informing me about a problem at the practice and it'd really help us—me—Sel—if you could drop it off."

I study him for a minute and concede on the grounds of how sweaty he is from the effort he's put in so far. Pipes bang again as I refill for a second cup.

"I can do it," I tell him.

"Seriously? Don't you have work today?"

"No, only a meeting later."

"That'd be great if you could help Louise, thanks."

As he hands over the envelope he gives me this look like he's wondering if it's such a good idea after all. After a moment weighing up his priorities, he releases the parcel—about as heavy as half the White Pages—then heads to the fridge to see what Selby has left him.

The Beluga clipping is at knee level on the left. He doesn't look at it or say a thing about it. Instead, he peers into the opening of an orange juice carton while I check the integrity of the envelope seal—it's well secured. He drinks straight from the carton and I swear off orange juice indefinitely. He puts the carton back in the fridge door.

"You don't have to go in or anything. Do you want me to tell you the bus route?"

"What is it?"

He searches a small pocket on his bag and pulls out a folded piece of paper.

"Take the 48 until Uscray, then it's the first left down Halifax. The building is number 10—the Caledonian. Apartment four is where you're going. Down the white stone path, into the courtyard, and halfway down on your left are some steps to the basement. Apartment four. There's a mailbox opposite the door. Just leave it in there."

"No, I mean what's in the envelope?"

"Oh. I don't know—a project or something. All I know is it's gotta be there by five."

He starts reloading his backpack—sans banana—then zips it up and swings it over his shoulder, adjusting the straps like he's ready to jump. He looks between me and the puddle beneath me which continues to expand drip by drip.

"So you know where you're going?"

I nod and go for my third refill.

"The address is right on it."

He heads out of the kitchen showing me the back of his hand in some sort of farewell gesture, then pauses in the doorway.

"What's your meeting for?"

"What meeting?"

"You said you had a meeting."

"Oh right. It's a research project."

"Researching what?"

"Don't know yet—that's the topic of the meeting."

He's standing there, insisting on eye contact, like he's trying to permeate my mind and lock in the details.

"Remember, five o'clock. That part is important."

STOP #1

The transit zone of the Pearson lab possesses a time measure of its own and it's not working in my favour. From where I'm sitting, the fifth-floor equivalent two blocks over seems like a much more peaceful place to reside. The windows glow a warm yellow like they're doing colour therapy, and I can almost tune into the soft cello that's almost certainly playing as they work. This is all speculation of course, and as hard as I try, these figments of serenity aren't strong enough to drown out the poorly researched account detailing the splintered life of a girl named Mary which takes place behind me.

From what I've gathered so far, there are a few important details to note about Mary:

1. She'll suggest plans like running a half-marathon, then stop training a week after paying the registration fee claiming ankle soreness.

2. She'll apply for jobs only to cancel the interviews.

3. One day her hair will be so smooth you could see the stars in it, and the next it'll be mainly horizontal because she failed to remove the hair tie after swimming.

4. She'll go out and speak not.

5. On Wednesday, Mary will be extremely excited about Thursday's plans, but come follow through, she'll be as enthused as a week-old balloon.

6. She'll say she's had enough and then pick fries off her friend's plate.

7. She'll stand firm on a point, and moments later she'll convert passively into submission like all her bones evaporated.

Apparently the constant uncertainty was too much for Mary's boyfriend, so he left her. Her hair did not benefit.

At times like this, I find it beneficial to imagine my immediate vicinity from a birds-eye view of so that I can:

a) calculate a safe distance from the confines of this kind of small-minded analysis and,

b) determine the best means of escape.

The lift involves waiting but minimal exertion. The stairs involve getting closer to them before I can get far away.

These two girls—women—what-have-you—are sitting behind me in the not-so-far opposite corner of the transit zone between the east and west wing of the Pearson lab, and I imagine, for some reason, they both want what the other has for lunch.

"She's clearly isolated herself. She doesn't see anyone, that's the problem."

"Has anyone told her?"

"Even if you tell her straight to her face she doesn't want to hear it. She'll hear something else."

"If she's ready to hear it, she'll hear it."

"It's just hard to watch."

After a short silence one of them finally finds the appropriate volume for the environment, but unfortunately the reprieve is short-lived.

"Hello? Excuse me?"

Their attention on the back of my neck engage my handlebar shoulders to maximum solidity.

"Excuse me? You over there in the tie-dye? Are you listening in on our conversation?"

I ignore the comment completely. My hope is they'll think I can't hear them and will resume their conversation in a more considerate tone.

My hopes are quickly dashed.

"It's pretty obvious you can hear me. You just snorted out a laugh and you've been nodding along since we got here."

With scapegoats limited, I turn to find two unimpressed expressions directed at me. Their legs are crossed so tight it enhances the centralised pinch between their brows.

"Sorry? Did you say something?"

"Do you have something you'd like to contribute?"

She's really expecting an answer, both of them are, but from where I'm sitting there is absolutely no way this could end well. My best bet is to state the obvious and hope they'll understand later when they have a quiet moment alone without so many pressing issues to discuss.

"I just think it's extremely likely Mary can feel your opinions. You might be underestimating her awareness."

As the echo of my words play back, chrome light spreads over their miffed expressions. It feels like a lot of time passes and no-one has done anything.

Lift or stairs?

Lift or stairs?

I'm half way across the transit area when the beige doors burst open to the west wing and this Leonardo guy appears in his white coat. His sharp-looking face reminds me why I'm on the fifth floor of the Pearson lab in the first place.

He looks at me, then at the other two, then back to me trying to get a sense of what he's walked into. His weight shifts to each foot as he holds the door open.

"We're ready for you now Louise. You can come through."

It's exactly the escape I hoped for.

—◇—

Leonardo walks two metres ahead of me with his toes turned outwards like they're presenting the office doors before they become fully visible. Fluorescents blast overhead, one replacing the next. It smells like hand sanitizer and re-circulated air.

Midway down the corridor he slows to a halt, extending his left arm toward an open door as if to say—*this is the lab, please enter*.

At about five degrees cooler the transit area encounter slides right off, and the room is dark too, which is lovely. It gets even better when he flicks a switch and blue and green lights extend over the glossy surfaces and anything metallic. It's cool, refreshing and calm. At least, it is until half the air leaves the room when I realise the whole right wall is actually a mirror. A girl in sweat soaked tie-dye is looking mad to see me. She's still got wind in her hair and her eyebrows take on directions of their own design.

"Is that a two-way mirror?" I ask Leonardo. He's studying the pages of the application I'd filled out during the early stages of the Mary synopsis. As he walks his coat flies out behind him like a cape.

"Yeah, it is."

He stops at the desk on the back end of the room and sits down heavily so the chair slides back about a metre. He pulls himself into his desk, eyes never deviating from the page.

"Does it do that thing where it dissolves away and you can see through it?"

"No, it doesn't. Have a seat Louise."

The only other chair available resembles that of a dentist's chair in an upright position. It faces the mirror and in front of it is a glass-top desk. Above the desk is this metal frame which is as wide as the desk and twice as high and suspended from it is a mechanical arm aparatus. I suspect it has something to do with why I'm here.

I arrange myself into the chair, watching Leonardo reading my answers in the reflection. He moves the pen down the page as he reads.

"You didn't tick the box about whether you were a student here?"

"No, not a student."

"Really?" He looks up at me and realises I'm looking at him in the mirror.

"Have you done this study before?"

"Nope."

After a moment cross-referencing my features, Leonardo rolls from behind the desk to my left side, he then presses a button and the desk top comes to life, glowing electric blue.

"Do you know much about the study, Louise?"

"I know nothing of it."

He types log-in details with one finger.

"Basically it's motor control test. What we're looking at is perception in relation to motion."

Leonardo looks up to see whether I understand the concept of perception in relation to motion.

"You mean like time loops?"

His blackened eyes look steady into mine. "Not quite."

After pressing Enter he slides to my right side, then unhooks the mechanical arm so it glides down in front of me, then situates the handle so it's within arms reach.

"The task is very simple. You simply grab this handle and push it away from you following the speed of a line that will appear on this screen. It should come on any second now."

He leans around me to press a button the keyboard and we both watch the screen—no change. In the reflection I notice a crayon drawing of a tree on the other side of the room.

"Kids aren't afraid of pressing really hard are they?"

Leonardo looks around because he doesn't know what I'm talking about, then this beep sounds and a yellow line about an inch thick flashes up on the screen at the end closest to me. A black dot appears in the centre of the line.

"Ok good." Leonardo exhales relief. "So it's going to look something like this."

He presses Enter again and a quieter beep sounds, then the line starts moving to the other end of the screen at about the speed it'd take a trombone player to make a 'woo-oop' sound. A second later, the line replaces itself at the start, and the dot resets itself too.

"So, if you grab the handle..."

I grab the handle.

"Now, imagine you're the black dot. You push the arm like it's an extension of you, and you're trying to keep the dot within the line. It's quite smooth and responsive. Try it."

He releases the handle and I take over. Leonardo's right—it's very responsive. I push too fast, way too fast. The dot and the line separate instantly.

"There'll be six rounds of one minute with two minutes in between. You can practice to get used to the weight of it, we're just waiting on my assistant."

I try again but go too fast, way too fast.

"You must be so good at this."

He doesn't respond. He's back at his desk with my form in his hand, pen moving down the paper again.

"What's the medical condition in your family that you ticked yes to?"

"I ticked yes?"

"Yes, you ticked yes."

"I meant no. No medical conditions."

The yellow line goes on its own now, beep after beep.

"What is it you're trying to achieve here?" I ask him.

"Are you asking me what we're researching?"

"Yes."

"We're looking at repetitive stress injuries. People who have certain lifestyle ailments from repeating certain motions again and again. We hope it'll give us a better idea of how we can treat people from an occupational therapy standpoint."

"Repetitive stress hey?" I let go of the handle and the dot disappears. "Can I ask you something?"

He doesn't look up. Eyes set on the form.

"You get a hundred dollars."

"No, it's not that. I was just wondering, do you ever get that feeling where you turn the tap on and you realise it's you who's been pulling it out of the wall all these years?"

Leonardo doesn't answer me, in fact, he looks pissed that I asked. Both his elbows hit his desk, fingertips to forehead, head shaking between them.

"This isn't going to work Louise."

"What? Why? Because I asked about the tap? You don't have to answer that."

"No, because you smoked marijuana in the last six months. Or did you tick that box wrong too?"

His eyes are darker now, stoic and disapproving with no colour variation between his pupil and iris. We're locked in a stare so much so these little blue shapes appear in his right eye, reflections of the two screens on his left. They're gone in a split second because he's suddenly rolling across the room towards a filing cabinet where he gets up and retrieves a folder. Scenes of him shoving rehab brochures in my face play out like a hologram between us.

"It was barely a hoot of hash an age ago. A puff-puff-pass scenario, you know how it is?"

Turns out, Leonardo didn't know how, and he didn't care to consider it either. Instead, he rolls back over to his desk to tear up my information, putting it in a cardboard box by my feet marked *recycling*.

Just as I'm about to breach the topic of the validity of his sample selection, particularly with regards to RSI where people were likely smoking a hoot of hash now and then to ease their discomfort, one of Mary's non-friends arrives, so I thought it best to leave.

EN ROUTE

I run into Amina on the way out. It's absolutely the perfect antidote. The Dahar twins are two of the few people I know who make it easy to step out of a bad mood. Catching even one of them for a minute is a potent remedy to any level of discomfort. I figure it has something to do with the accent; the altered inflection igniting different neural pathways that bring new life to the same old conversations.

She's leaving the library and I'm heading to the footpath when we intersect. The amorous way she greets me does well to delete that whole waste of an hour, and the speed of her speech forces my full attention.

"Please tell me you've seen the error of your ways and you're re-enrolling?"

"I can only tell you I've seen the error of my ways."

It's bright out, over-saturated. Half her face is lit gold and the other half is shadowed by the library building so she's got one light brown eye and one jet black one. Her dark hair does an interpretive dance in the hot wind and she doesn't work to tame it. She looks down at the parcel between my wrist and thigh, worn at the corners from the journey so far.

"What's with the envelope?"

"I'm on a delivery mission," I explain, following her lead down the paved steps so we're about to merge with the torrent of foot traffic.

"Is it an urgent mission?" She asks. "I'm heading home and I know Amal would benefit from a familiar face, and also, I have a riddle for you."

"I love riddles. Let me get my bike."

Walking with Amina is like pure immersion in another world; everything rushes by, people don't have faces, and somehow passing objects illuminate to amplify her stories, like how the curve of the old man's spine walking six shuffles to every one of our strides highlights how her inherited back pain has flared up of late, and how, when she mentions home, I'm looking into a pub and the TV blasts a news anchor with slick flat hair and bright red lips—neither of which would last in this heat.

Despite her ailment, Amina's two paces ahead of me at most times, carving through the crowds while I piss people off because my bike takes up too much room and no-one wants it on the footpath. She's telling me about a date gone wrong and I'm practically running to hear.

"So we're sitting there at this family diner and he's is asking about my family and work and school, but he's so bored Lou, watching my responses fly over the table like a glow-in-the-dark shuttlecock, so I'm thinking *what the hell even motivated me to come here in the first place?* And then it dawned on me."

Her story halts because she's calculating a gap in traffic. Our heads turn left, right, then left again and she darts across the road and so I do too, cutting off a cyclist marginally but sufficiently enough for him to give me the finger and call me a fucker.

"You're the fucker!" Amina retorts, then she helps me with my bike so we can run up the stairs to her go-to deli. I park it on the deli side of the concrete pillar, out of view for the most part, and we're soon enveloped by a refrigerated realm of air conditioned comfort which refreshes my hotspots and excites a shiver.

When the blue haze subsides, the shopkeeper emerges. He's mid full-body scan on us and doesn't look very impressed with the results. Everything settles into its final colour and Amina leads the way over the dusty concrete floor through the aisles of packaged goods and hand-written price tags. A familiar song crackles over the speaker, the static interupting identification.

"So what did you realise?" I ask her as she ventures down the chip aisle.

"Oh, I realised I'm wasting my time thinking I have to do shit like that."

She grabs some two packets and heads for the counter, and we arrive three deep in the line behind a couple while the shopkeep searches for a certain brand of cigarettes for the ponytailed man first in line.

"But it's wine number three, time is purging, the bar is three shades dimmer and we both know where this is going."

"And did it?"

Amina nods and reaches into her backpack, presumably for some method of payment. The interest emanating from the couple in front of us is tangible. Ponytail leaves with his smokes so we're next.

"Must be some sort of cultural variance or something Lou, because next thing I know we're back at his place and he's flipping me here, flipping me there and all I can think is, *Oh god, my back. Please, Allah, don't hurt my back.*"

The couple in front reluctantly depart with their cat food and rice crackers and we take their place at the counter. Shopkeep has an excellent poker face, exhibiting no emotive responses to Amina's story whatsoever. She lays the chips on the counter, asks for a lighter and some papers, then sets a twenty on the counter.

"Do you think you've recovered?"

"Physically—I've been better. Emotionally—I can't tell. Mentally—I'm adrift."

I take the chips and she gets her change and the lighter and we're out the door.

"I haven't heard from him since, so I guess he didn't have a nice time either."

"It really could be anything," I tell her.

Amina sets the pace again. We dodge up-ended pavers, weave through pedestrians and I run over a man's toe but don't look back to see his reaction. Ruthless, I know.

One and a half blocks later, I catch up and she helps me with my bike up the steps to her building. The glass doors part and another realm of chill welcomes us. Amina presses in her four digit code in the panel on the right, then this dulled buzz sounds and the next set of doors open to the lobby where a doorman sits reading a newspaper. She nods to him and he smiles back, then his smile reduces when he notices the condition of my bike.

"So what do you think?" she asks.

"About what?"

"About my riddle?"

"Oh, I can't explain it."

"C'mon Lou, I need guidance."

"Uh-uh. The last decent rapport I had with a man was a fresh-out-of-uni chemist who sold me the morning after pill a couple of months back. You're asking the wrong person."

I leave my bike in the storage room next to the mailboxes. The next closest lift is on the sixth floor. Amina presses the up button.

"That's what I miss about home man. There's no bullshit in a third world country. It's life or death, every day. You say what you mean. None of this fluff."

"But then your line of study would be rendered useless, wouldn't it?"

"That would not be a problem," she smiles. "Listen to me, I've been talking non-stop about these trivial matters. I haven't even asked you what you're doing now?"

Fourth floor.

Third floor.

"There's not much to tell really. I bike around, loiter in dimly lit places, sit in parks—activities in that vain."

Amina releases her bag to her feet and starts rolling her head side to side to stretch her neck.

"Sounds relaxing."

Second floor.

"I mustn't be explaining it right then."

First floor.

The lift doors open to present this sun-kissed guy emanating a casual, foreign flavour—the kind that can pull off the recently-rolled-out-of-bed-curls-and-holiday-wear ensemble that would render a less flavoursome commoner, like myself, slack and good-for-nothing. An acquaintance of the Dahar's apparently. Amina introduces him as Tanzania, or perhaps she says he's from Trinidad—I miss that part wondering what the trophy sticking out of his backpack celebrated.

"What's the trophy for?" Amina asks as we exchange places, turning to face him in the lobby. She presses the 10 button and just as it looks like we won't find out the answer, he leaps in with inches to spare. He's on my left side. Amina on my right. Half a foot separates us and the doors seal us in.

"Spelling bee."

"Seriously? What was your word?"

"Indolence."

Amina looks to the grey paneled roof for answers.

"I-n-d-o-l-e-n-c-e."

"I think the more important question is what was *his* word and how many people are involved in this club."

"Ah, fair point," she concedes. "What was his word?"

"Amygdala."

"That seems unfair."

"I agree, but then, it's just for fun and to learn the language so we didn't fight about it too much."

"And you were the victor."

"That I was," he smiles proudly. "But tell me, how was Cambodia?"

"Brilliant. I loved every minute of it." She looks at me. "You would've loved it too Lou; all these revolutionaries, working for change. Those people, man, they're my kind of people. We talked free speech and politics and drank every night. Everyday man, that's what they do—that's what they live."

"Sounds amazing," Tanzania's fixated on her, watching as she stretches out her neck.

Amina notices him noticing. "Didn't you just come from up here?"

"I did. I was visiting your brother. He seems well."

Her mood instantly dips and she gives him a deadened look.

"You're joking right? He hasn't left the apartment in two weeks."

The lift stops at 10 and we wait the obligatory fourteen counts for the doors to open. When they do, I follow her out.

"Come to the Esther Friday night, ladies. I'll put you on the door."

"Alright. Friday—The Esther."

"You'll actually come this time, right?"

"Of course, of course."

He offers a farewell salute which Amina doesn't see then winks at me and retreats back into the lift. The doors close and grey walls and burgundy carpet outline our path.

"Is that true?" I ask her.

"Yeah. Well, no, not really. He asks every week but I never go."

"No, I mean is that true about Amal not leaving the apartment in two weeks?"

She sighs. "I told you Lou—he's turning sour."

STOP #2

Tanzania was being kind, Amal does not look well at all. His cheeks are soufflèd like he hasn't smiled in months and he's got tired eyes like he just woke up from a face-first slumber. The sight of chips impresses him somewhat, and he stands aside to let us pass.

"Is your back causing you trouble too?" I ask as I enter.

"My back always hurts," Amal says. "It's a curse of the family."

It's cool inside, dark too. The curtains are pulled so the only light is what creeps through from the space above and below. Amina takes a swift right into the kitchen.

"Does anyone want a drink?"

I accept, Amal says nothing, but he does follow me into the living room where ghost versions of myself from previous visits splay across the furniture, alongside ghost versions of the oscillating groups who linger around them, milking their good nature.

Amal overtakes me and falls into the three-seater couch, settling in horizontally. He's certainly seen better days. His slippered feet hang off the edge, tapping a song only he can hear. I sit on the one-seater perpendicular to his feet.

"What's with the envelope?" he asks in precisely the same tone as Amina asked.

"It's for Selby." I look around the living room for a clock. "Do you know what time it is?"

"I'd guess about two."

"Yeah, it feels about two."

One litre later, Amina spins in with a glass of water for each of us. She sits on the other side of the coffee table so we're in an isosceles formation, then she picks up a pack of smokes and slides one out.

"How is Selby?" she asks. "Is she still doing those awesome map drawings?"

"She's alright. No, not so much. She's more into theatre now."

Amina's nodding, processing the information and trying for ignition but the lighter just sparks. Three times — no luck. She looks between me and Amal.

"That's the third time that old flannel man has sold me a dud. I swear he keeps the rejects just for me." She shakes her head in distaste and pushes herself up to her feet. "Is everyone happy with the snack selection? You guys want anything else?"

We don't want anything else, so she heads for the door. When it closes, Amal starts tapping his foot to a song only he can hear and looks at me through barely open eyes. It's not until she's gone that the starkness of the apartment becomes apparent. It's bleak, stagnant and stale. Even the painting of the old red Pontiac amongst the palms looks different. The neon yellow sign in the background glowing 'Libre Nation' seems to've blown a fuse.

"Sorry Amina dragged you up to this tenth-floor dungeon Lou Lou."

"Don't be," I counter. "I needed a rest-stop. I've got a long commute. Plus, I like it here. The darkness is refreshing."

"I'll at least open a window for you."

With some effort, Amal rolls himself upright and heads to the balcony door, pushing both curtains to the left side so he can slide it open all the way. He looks out to the neighbouring building a block over.

"It's so hot," he moans. "It's not even officially summer yet."

"It is a bit bullshit."

"These guys are playing Wii Tennis."

He juts with his chin to the neighbouring building then looks at me to see if I'm paying attention. He's backlit with dust hovering around his outline like the motes are long time acquaintances.

"Where have you been Lou Lou? I haven't seen you in ages."

I consider his question as I slide from the one-man couch to the floor for better leverage in accessing anything to fidget with—in this case: the Rubik's Cube sitting on the edge of the ashtray. He picks up a cigarette pack and bumps one out, then remembers the lighter situation and puts it back in.

"I wish I had something to tell you my friend, but there aren't too many highlights on this reel. Just lots of the same pictures in an almost perfect rotation."

He looks back outside, first to his neighbours, then down to the street below.

"I should warn you Habibi, Jimmy and Hazif are on their way, so if you want to dodge them you have a ten-to-twenty-minute window to vacate."

"Thanks for the heads up. Their presence isn't a bother though."

He shuffles his slippered feet next to me so he's standing about three times taller than me from this angle. He offers his hand to assist me up.

"Come. I wanna show you something."

Amal's room is big enough to house a double bed, a side table and a chest of drawers that he could probably only open about three-quarters of the way. Faded dark blue bed linen and grey walls make up the colour scheme. They're bare except for one poster of a heavy chested lady that looks like it's been folded many times. The blinds are shut and one illuminated lightbulb hangs in the centre of the room.

"Lay down and close your eyes."

My expression earns me an eye-roll. He turns off the light and flops on the bed. "I'm not being weird, I swear."

"Famous last words."

"Are your eyes closed? Keep them closed."

"They're closed."

"Are you laying down?"

"No, I haven't moved at all."

"You can stand if you want, but you'll want to be laying down in about thirty seconds."

I feel for the edge lay back so I'm upper torso on, knees and shins off. I've stopped breathing and I'm sure he's noticed. Neons shapes morph behind my eyes, reds, then blues turning to green.

"Are your eyes shut?"

"Yes."

"Okay, you can open them now."

I do and the full spherical volume of my eyeballs softens because across the roof is another light show, of constellations—glimmering white stars, bright in some sections, dulled in others. Always in motion. Patterns of shimmer lit against the black.

"They're LEDs," he tells me. "Took ages to fix them just right."

"You made this?"

The bed moves indicating a nod.

"They're enmeshed in netting and automated through my phone. I think it works because it's not flush against the roof. I pulled sections down at the sides and corners so it's curved, like the shape of your eye. Phase two is to introduce another level, maybe two more. I haven't got there yet. Ran out of steam."

He starts tapping his foot again. I feel the warmth of him about a foot away. A static of considered distance travels between us.

"When we were little my dad used to take us camping. We'd lie on the sand and he'd point out constellations and tell us these stories. He said if you focused on them long enough, you could superimpose them on your body and they would merge with you and diffuse any worries you had in the moment."

How lovely.

"I know a guy who has a similar theory about birds."

"Oh yeah?"

"Does it work for you?"

 "Sometimes. If it's quiet enough."

A shooting star crosses from left to right. One area brightens, another section fades out.

"The way my eyes feel when I look at this makes me happy."

"Oh yeah? That's good." He seems pleased with himself. I can feel him smiling. I find myself doing the same at the thought of a miniature Amal and Amina spread eagled in the desert looking at the stars during a simple, more innocent time of their lives.

"I lied before Lou, when I said I haven't seen you in ages."

"When did you see me?"

"Weeks ago. At Greenmere Park. You were reading."

"What was I reading?"

His foot tapping stops.

"I don't know, but you looked mad."

"That's just what my face looks like. Why didn't you say hello?"

"I was on the bus."

"Oh, fair enough."

The tapping starts back up.

"As you can tell, I've very unemployed."

"I think this is a great use of your time."

"Amina thinks I'm depressed."

"What? Why does she think that?"

"Because I don't do much and because I'm not particularly happy."

"Why aren't you happy?"

"I don't know." He stretches out, then deflates. "No job. No motivation. I don't know. I might be in denial, but I'm not depressed."

As another cluster brightens it sounds like he's about to say something else, but he stops himself and shifts instead.

"What?"

"What what?"

"You were going to say something."

"It's just something else she said."

"About what?"

"Why you quit school."

"Oh."

"Why did you do that?"

I shake my head but can't tell if he registers the movement.

"I don't know really, it just wasn't for me anymore."

"You only had one semester left."

"Yeah, and I don't know how I let myself get that far."

A section travels from corner to corner so I try to superimpose the bright spots over my tense spots when they pass over me, but all I can feel are my handlebar shoulders and they're gone before any relief comes.

"There's gotta be something to it?" he presses.

"There really isn't." Now my foot starts up. *How to explain it?* "Your sister—they need. She's a natural, and when you see that contrast, it makes it even more clear."

"You can't compare though."

"It's not comparing like, *oh, I suck compared to her*, it's more like, *that's an able person, she's got some steady ground beneath her and that could really help a person*. She has this confidence about her."

"That's what they want," he sighs. "Confidence."

"Well, maybe I don't mean confidence, it's more like... she doesn't see a difference between anyone, so it's easy for her to ask whatever she wants because to her, we're all on the same level, and that gives her so much brain space, so much room to move. Or at least, that's what it looks like from where I'm standing."

"She's got the tourist's mentality."

"She really does. It's not like she thinks deserves anything more than someone else, but if she doesn't know, she'll ask, and really, what else can you do? I don't know, I think that can help a person. She has this way about her. An ease."

"I wish that gene was dispersed more evenly."

"Oh, I know."

"So what's your plan?"

"My plan is to have a plan."

Three knocks at the front door permeate our homemade cosmos and makes the bed feel like a bed again. My focus shifts and the proximity of the four walls become apparent.

"Patience, I guess, young Habibi."

Three more knocks and Amal's name rings through too.

"Maybe they've got the answers we need?"

"I doubt it," he breathes, edging off the bed. "All they've got are questions."

INFLUENCE

One minute I'm orbiting space and the next I'm back at the foot of the one-seater couch with Hazif on the seat behind me. He's unconcerned with our close proximity despite near-stranger status.

Jimmy's sprouted sideburns since I last saw him. He's sitting on the other one-man couch by Amal's head. Jimmy and Hazif have the kind of relationship where they bicker like an old couple.

"Do you know how many meals I cooked today?" Hazif asks, stretching out like he's just been released from confinement.

"Let me guess—three hundred?" Jimmy responds.

"That's right. Three hundred. Three hundred lunch plates. Do you realise how intense that is? Plus I woke up at 5am to run up the mountain. What'd you do all day?"

"Literally nothing. I do nothing. I have no idea what my job role is. I can't imagine what they think of me."

Amal's slipper is tapping at high speed, no longer a song, more like some morse code message that I really need to hear.

"How much have you smoked today man?" Hazif eyes Amal up and down.

"Nothing, I haven't smoked at all."

"Yeah? Smells another story. You look like Jimmy that night he took the horse tranquilizer."

Jimmy shoots Hazif a death stare, who in turn, produces a thin joint which he's pointing in Jimmy's direction. Jimmy's looking at him like he's considering going in for a neck-kill.

"You gotta keep bringin' that up man? I took it one time and fell asleep straight away."

Amal rolls to his side and looks at Jimmy as wide-eyed as he can manage.

"You fell asleep straight away?"

"Let's not get into that now, okay?" Jimmy's expression insists Amal shut up. He did have the advantage, because of Amal's incapacitation.

"Amal—let's call your guy. My guy's gone missing. This my last crumb."

Amal flips himself so he's on his back again, hands behind his head, elbows out wide. His slipper hangs on by sock lint. I replace it for him and he smiles *thanks.*

"He just left. You probably passed him in the hall."

"You're kidding?"

"I'm not kidding. I don't kid anymore."

"Did you buy any?"

"No." Amal's forearm covers his face. "I just like talking to him."

"Can we call him back?"

"No, it's too late." He rolls on his side and closes his eyes. "I know his dad's in prison, I know his sister's in med school dating a guy name Bank and I know he used to be an Olympian in his youth. He comes here at least onces a month just to say hi, but his name—nope. Couldn't tell ya."

Hazif switches to Arabic for a sentence or two and Amal stiffens and Jimmy look stunned in response. "Look at you man, you gotta get up and do something.

You lay here all day, too much time to think and you're thinking your way down a funnel. Your sister's starting to worry."

Amal's bolt upright—the quickest I've seen him move since I arrived. His jaw locked, nostrils flaring. Pot smoke wafts across the coffee table.

"I am *doing something*," Amal releases, his tone measured, just below breaking point. "I make the fuckin' calls, I fill out every fucking dot point. I dress up and put on the demeanour, I do it all and it's not enough."

"Try something else then, anything, something so you're not sitting stagnant in this apartment. It's just a reality of life man. Everyone does it."

Amal's chewing potential responses and it looks like he's having trouble swallowing. He slumps back into the couch.

"You don't get it."

"Then explain it to me."

Amal shakes his head too tired to bother. I don't blame him either. His book is now closed. I can practically hear him wishing he was in his room with fewer judgments and more stars.

Jimmy's fingers form into a pyramid between his knees.

"I know what you mean though," he offers in mediation. "My friend Jace graduated from engineering three years ago and present day, he's delivering pizza."

"*Great.*" Amal breathes.

Hazif takes another hoot before leaning over me, then the coffee table to offer it to Jimmy, who meets him halfway.

"You're both looking at it all wrong," Hazif says on his descent. "It's not like it's gonna be this clear cut job title, this definitive thing that's going to solve everything—it's more what you bring to it. Times are changing man. Someone needs a sous chef and I need a job—it's symbiotic. And besides, the skills you learn are transferable. They'll come in useful later for something, you just don't know what it is yet."

"And what does symbiotic mean for those who aren't aware?" Jimmy's holding his intake. His eyes glisten as the high circulates within.

"Symbiotic? It's a mutually beneficial relationship. I need money and they're giving away money in exchange for my time. Symbiosis."

Jimmy exhales and softens into the couch, smiling wide like an all-knowning sage.

"You know who would be perfect for this discussion?" He looks between all of us on his own time. No-one replies. "Harris Parchment."

"Jimmy—who the fuck is Harris Parchment?" Hazif asks. "You've been doing this the whole way over, saying ambiguous things like that."

Jimmy inhales again and holds the joint out to Amal who then passes it straight to me. I take it from it and study the ember where Leonardo dwells, judging me, smoke billowing from his head.

"How to explain Harris Parchment?" Jimmy wonders through the haze. "The man handles the art of parlay with grace like no other. He's got an answer to everything—a legend of his time. It's hard to explain what it is about him, and even harder to explain what happened to him last semester."

Amal rolls himself upright again, moving like jelly. He heads toward the balcony door and opens it the width of him. I pass the joint to Hazif.

"Well you're going to have to now after that introduction." Amal says.

"He fully inverted everything."

"What do you mean *he inverted everything*?" Hazif asks, lungs full.

"He flipped it—all of it. Night is day. Yes is no. Quit school. Quit his job at the gym. I was there the day he did it—spinning the whole thing to his boss with this spaced-out look on his face, like Buddha or something. Completely blissin'."

"Like he took a horse tranquilizer?" Amal asks.

Jimmy contemplates violence, again, and again, he decides better of it.

"What'd he say?" I ask him.

"What's that now?"

"At the gym, what'd he say to his boss?"

"That he's seen it."

"Seen what?"

"Don't remember exactly. The light, probably. He was talking in his trade-mark circles and I was on the elliptical. And it was hot."

"Which gym?"

"Hudson Downtown." Jimmy looks bright and alert all of a sudden, moving forward to the edge of his seat. "Why so interested?"

"He just sounds like someone I know, that's all."

There's a knock at the door and we all look to Amal. He's lazy in his movement, slippers barely leaving the carpet. Jimmy's studying me, eyes small and speculative.

"So what are you doing now Louise? Still studying?"

Before I can tell him about the training, Amina appears with a pizza man in tow. He's got a box in his hand and a hat on his head and then this musical conversation ensues with lyrics too quick for me to distinguish. My name is the only discernible word, repeated twice in the time it takes everyone to resume their position around the coffee table.

Amina lights her cigarette.

Jace stays until the end of the joint.

He certainly didn't seem too dissatisfied with delivery life the way his cheeks held an almost permanent smile, but I doubt he knew where he was going when he left.

STOP #3

From an outsiders perspective, everything would appear exactly the same. Glenn's on duty dealing with a potential new client, Tyrone's coaching a girl into a deep squat, then out of a deep squat, and next to me a girl is struggling hard against the StairMaster looking desperately unhappy and equally unstable.

"So, you're keen on Tyrone?"

Although she's looking straight ahead it's clear she's addressing me. Her ponytail whips in an almost perfect nine to three motion and she's at triple my speed but it seems more like the machine's working her.

"Don't worry. I get it. That's what I'm doing here too." She gives me a sidewards glance. "Not Tyrone though. He's got nice arms, I'll give him that. I'm here for Glenn."

Tyrone looks up as soon as she says that, proving that if one talks about someone loud enough in a wide open space, they'll soon notice.

He nods a single upward motion to acknowledge my presence and continues his supervisor role watching for form, precision and a general good time.

"You should've been here last year when Lloyd Sumner worked here. Can you even believe it? Lloyd Sumner—in these walls—just one year ago. They were the good old days. Monday and Wednesday mornings and Friday nights."

The very memory puts extra pace in her strides. She takes a sip from her floral pink water bottle as she eyes me up and down.

"You have really excellent muscle definition," she says this as she replaces her bottle then tightens her ponytail. "What's your routine? All cardio? Do you integrate yoga? Because I hear that's necessary. "

"I don't exercise," I tell her. "I just over-analyze everything."

"Oh god." Her gaze drops to the floor in front of her. "He's coming over. Oh god. Do you think he heard me say his name before? *Shit!*"

With every step he takes in our direction, Tyrone's client reduces her squat depth by inches. By the time he's in front of my treadmill, her weights are on the floor.

"Lou Lou, where you been girl? And hell, what's this pace? Two point two?"

"Two point zero." I correct him.

"Are you pushing a newborn down Westwood on a Sunday with your nanna who's dead? It's at least a five in my gym."

"Five is a young girl's game and this isn't your gym."

"In my mind it is. Still gotta exercise you know, even if the main attraction's gone."

Tyrone reaches over to press the up arrow so I put one foot either side of the conveyer belt which goes on without me. He concedes with hands up as if to say, *fine—be sedentary*, and I press on the down arrow until it's moving at a more leisurely pace for re-entry.

"Like I said—a young girls game."

"Why the absense? You've got greys it's been so long."

"I do not."

"You do, I can see them."

I glare at him. At least he finds himself funny.

"You spoke to my boy lately?"

"Nope, not lately."

Tyrone notices my footwear and frowns.

"Best on ground again last week. That's four weeks running. Better give me props for all that PT time—"

Tyronne is cut off by the significant grunt exerted by Ponytail. She's pulled the emergency stop so she's freeze-framed mid run eyes wide and disbelieving.

"Wait a minute—who's your boy?"

"Harris Parchment," I tell her, then turn to Tyrone. "Does he still work here?"

Tyrone looks back to his client who's watching us in the mirror. He smirks at me, then stretches both arms overhead.

"I see what you did there, you got that loyalty, I like that."

"*You* know Lloyd Sumner?" Ponytail is still coming to terms with the information. Tyrone tilts his head. His ear almost flush with his enhance trap.

"Everyone does, Lorraine, relax."

Ponytail's heat splotches melt together at Tyrone's mention of her name, prompting her to concerns herself with some buttons. The machine starts up again at a more breast friendly pace.

"What'd'ya wanna know about HP for? Don't tell me you're into that whimsical fairy."

"Whimsical fairy? No, I'm not into him. Can't anyone just enqu—I'm supposed to interview him, for a paper."

He looks disbelieving which is fair, since it's a blatant lie.

"To answer your question—yeah, he worked here, 'til he went psycho. Flipped out one day. We haven't seen him since."

"What do you mean *flipped out*?"

Tyronne shrugs.

"I don't know what to tell ya. Dude quit. No more class. Disappeared off the face of the Daily Planet like a wasp. What do ya wanna interview for anyway? Don't you want someone suave, like me? You can do whatever you want with me girl, I finish soon."

"Do you know how I can find him?"

He rolls his eyes, tired of the subjec, then shakes his head.

"Like I said—wasp. Last I heard was Glenn sayin' somethin' about him and a stint at the Mech Institute. But I'm tellin' ya Lou, you'd have more fun with me."

"Lucrative offer," I tell him. "One more thing—what's the best way to get to Uscray from here, by bike?"

REPLICA

The problem with maps is they don't show the third dimension. Even though Tyrone provided me with an aerial view of the bike path from downtown to Uscray, by the time I'd circled around memories of his phone screen, many a park bench and the residue of Zac's descriptors, the sun's shimmering just above the horizon indicating I'd missed the deadline.

Through much foliage and after two complete misses, I locate the steps to the basement area where it's white and cold and smells like chlorine, though, that could just be my smell bouncing off the walls.

Pipes line the roof. One door with the number 4 embossed on it, painted over for five coats at least.

The exact moment I press the doorbell I remember Zac's instructions about leaving the package in the mailbox, but before I can re-evaluate the situation, the door opens two inches and a small, tanned guy with a buzz cut and an X tattooed above his left eyebrow appears behind the silver chain. He waits for me to tell him what I want.

"Oh, hi. I... have a delivery for Alexis."

The door closes without a word. At first it seems like he's locking it in two places, but then it floats open to expose him halfway down the hall, basketball shorts glistening with every step.

"Come on in," he calls back, disappearing around a corner. "A-lex-ee. Compa-nee."

The hallway is lined with a series of collage photo frames; the kind with many different shaped photo opportunities in one convenient frame. They're mostly group shots; assortments of urban gangsters taken over the years. A broad-chested fellow features in most of them, I imagine him to be Alexis.

I'm contemplating apologizing for the incorrect pronunciation of his roommates name when X comes back into view. He's on the other side of the living space standing near the kitchen table behind the U-formation of couches. Since he's already preoccupied with dragging a chair across the room, I reconsider the need for an apology.

He stops underneath a small window on the far wall about a foot from the ceiling then stands on the chair. From there her pushes out the window which'd be equal to just above ground level, and because of the way the window opens, he can probably only see some of last years leaves and a few feet of grass.

The east wall has a door way to another hall and the wall covered with shelves, filled with books stacked end to end. Based on the colours of the spines, they're mostly horror/thriller/crime.

"Do you know what time it is?" X asks, bending and tilting his head for a better vantage point.

"I know, I'm sorry it's late."

He retreats back inside and looks at me, perplexed.

"What's late?"

Before I can answer his question this intense siren pierces, penetrating my brain folds like some form of torture. On the second ring I realize it's a home phone, and X jumps of the chair to answer it but some other figure beats him to it.

Framed by the kitchen counter top and the cabinets overhead is the torso of a shirtless guy; skinny yet muscular and not happy with the intrusion.

"For fucks-sake—he's gone. We've told you this a thousand times. Stop calling." And he slams the phone down.

Aaron's wide-eyed, then looks at me playfully, shaking his head to shake of the matter, then he heads back to his chair while this shirtless guy pours some cereal into a large blue salad bowl. He adds some milk, gets a spoon and stands on the other side of the kitchen table, looking at Aaron without acknowledging my presence at all. He has the same haircut as X and about a foot on him.

"It's not gonna happen today,"

"It might. You don't know." X rises to his toes. "What's your name girl?"

No-one says anything.

"He's talking to you." Cereal says to me.

"Me? My name?"

"Yes."

"Louise. My name is Louise"

Somewhere else in the apartment a door opens and a figure the shape of a rugby player or security guard makes his way from down the other hall, backlit by the toilet window. The number '13' glows white on his right peck. It turns out the whole household uses the same barber.

This guy's got a face tattoo too; along his jawbone it reads 'Family' in Old English.

"Hi?" He-who-must've-been-Alexis eyes my sweaty hairline like Zac did earlier but with significantly less disdain. He seems amused with the development ongoing in the living space and it takes me a moment to remember my place and the envelope weighing me down. I hold it out to him at about a seventy percent extension.

"This is from Selby."

He takes it off me.

"What's is it?"

"I have no idea."

"Did you try to open it?"

"No. Of course not."

Out comes a Swiss Army knife from Alexis' back pocket. While maintaining eye-contact he inserts the blade into the corner and slices it open. I think he's trying to look menacing, but it doesn't work. To me, the tattoo seems more like a greeting card—friendly and sincere.

"My name is Aaron, by the way." X tells me from the chair top.

From the envelope, Alexis withdraws a thick mass of paper, like an instruction manual of some kind, then heads next to Aaron to lean on the wall beside him. Without the height supplement he's only a few inches shorter.

"Sorry it's late," I tell him.

"It's not late," he says, flipping through the pages to the back section. "It's perfectly on time."

Aaron retreats inward from the opening so he's got a birds-eye view of the pages.

"What's that you got there, Lex?"

"Paper Mache Parasols," he muses.

"What the folly is Paper Mache Parasols?"

Alexis's too busy reading a passage on one of the last few pages to answer. Whatever he reads envokes a closed mouth laugh. The pages to fan to a close and he looks at me. It seems like the perfect time to start my journey toward the door.

"Okay, well, I'll be going now."

"Do you want to stay for an iceblock?"

"Do I want an iceblock?"

"Yeah."

"Uh.. okay..."

There's a subtlty to Alexis' blink which resembles a nod. He moves with grace passed the kitchen table and tosses the the document over the back of the couch. Aaron lands at the same time it does.

"Oh, of course—it's the script."

He sweeps by me and heads straight for it; leaping over the back of the couch, disappearing from view entirely.

Cereal is a distance away, watching all this unfold on the other side of the living room next to the bookshelf with the blue bowl at his chin. He motions the spoon toward Aaron.

"That's the script?"

"It's Paper Mache Parasols," Aaron answers matter-of-factly.

"Pass it here. I want to read it?"

"Nope." Alexis's response is firm and decided. He's elbow deep in the freezer shaped not too dissimilar to him. "You can come watch it though."

"I'm not watching it, just let me read it."

"That's a hard no D."

Cereal's mad, real mad. He retreats down the hall and a few seconds later, a door slams.

"Maybe I'll skip the iceblock," I say, backing away. "It's been nice to meet you both."

Aaron's quick to his knees, leaning on the back of the couch with the script between us.

"You goin'?"

"My work here is done."

"Stay for five and have an iceblock with us. Don't worry about Jarrad. He's just in a mood. He's not like that because you're here. It's a regular occurance."

He looks to where Cereal was standing then leans in like he's about to tell me a secret.

"He just pissed because the guy who wrote this play nailed his ass to the wall once. Not literally, of course, but he fried him in front of his whole class, so he's a bit touchy."

Alexis returns with three lemomade iceblocks, already unwrapped, and disperses them between us. Aaron leaps over the back of couch, rests the script on the couch back and heads for the window.

"Anyway, you have to stay. I don't care what D says, I reckon today's the day."

"Uh-uh." Alexis makes the sound with his iceblock between his front teeth while he carries a chair in each hand to set up near Aaron's. He removes the iceblock and sits on one, stretching his legs wide and resting his elbows on his quads.

"Definitely not going to happen today. I saw him before and he looked real morose."

Aaron's looks down at Alexis from the chairtop and hangs his head in defeat, jumping down, he sits on his chair in the same position as Alexis, who motions to the empty one. I concede with the hope that the longer I stay, the more their nonchalance for relative strangers rubs off on me.

The iceblock is cold and sweet. It's perfect.

"The day for what?" I ask as I sit.

"How rude of us." Aaron says, chewing. "Our neighbour—5D—is planning to propose to his girlfriend—5DD." He looks at Alexis and purses his lips. "Sorry—Evelyn. It's absolutely terrifying, Louise. Every Thursday, after he gets back from karate, they sit at the concrete table out there and talk about their day. She doesn't know it, but for like three months now he's been trying to rally the nerve to ask her, but she's always cutting him off right as he's about to do it."

"Terrifying? Really?" Alexis asks, smiling at his iceblock.

Aaron shivers in response then cups his forehead. Brain-freeze. He swallows heavy while the X folds as a result of his forehead wrinkles.

"I'm just so nervous for him," he says, squinting heavily. "I hate not know-ing."

The phone rings again—shrill and clinical. Exactly what brain-freeze would sound like if it had a corresponding tone.

"Speaking of not knowing, I'm gonna answer that, then I'm gonna read your script."

Aaron is spritely in his movements which I appreciate because I only have to endure one and a half rings of the awful sound. He answers the phone in a much friendlier manner.

"Yellow?"

"So, you live with Selby?" Alexis asks, biting off a chunk of his nearly fin-ished iceblock. A piece of mine falls in my lap. I pick it up and put it in my mouth.

"That's right. I do."

"So with Zac then too?"

"Yep. They're kind of a package deal."

"Were you the one living there with her when she lived with Lloyd Sumner?"

Aaron slams down the phone and the two of them exchange a look.

"Why can't we get the number changed?" Aaron asks, trudging back.

"You know why."

"I know he's old but couldn't we sort out speed dial for him? It'd be even less work on his part."

"He wont get it man. You know that."

Aaron swipes the script from the couch and returns to his chair, tending to some drips on the base of his iceblock that result from a moments neglect.

"What were you saying about Lloyd Sumner?"

"Louise used to live with him."

Aarons mood lightens significantly.

"Tell me everything. What's he like?"

I shrug. "He's exactly as you see him. TV makes him look smaller."

"Have you seen that billboard of him downtown? It's like six stories tall. My dad says he's probably the greatest export our city has ever seen."

"I wouldn't say that." I counter.

"I would. He's even bigger than you Lex."

Alexis looks preoccupied. He's finished his iceblock and now he's tapping his stick against his knee in a similar tempo to Amal and his slipper; another morse code message I'm too slow to translate. Alexis tilts his ear to the window like he's heard something outside. Aaron is silent, alert. We sit there, listening.

Obnoxious exhaust.

Succession of motorbikes.

Birds hooting.

Aaron shakes his head. "Not tonight."

"So Louise, are you a full-time delivery person or is it a casual gig?" Alexis asks as I finish my iceblock.

"Part-time."

"And the other part?" Aaron asks.

"Nothing of consequence. Lately I've been participating in medical research experiments."

Aaron stops analysing which part he's going to lick next and looks at me, deadpan.

"What do you mean *research experiments*?"

"You know, like, researchers testing hypotheses, collecting data—that kind of thing. It's not a very traditional source of income, but our place is rent controlled and I don't really need much."

Aaron looks at me like that's the best response I could've given him.

"What kind of stuff do they do to you? Do you get probed?"

"No, nothing that penetrative."

"What kind of stuff then?"

"I did one on sleep rhythms recently. That's really messed with me."

"How so?" Alexis asks.

"It was long—six days, five nights. Now my sleep cycles are ruined. Short ones are best. Hour long and non-invasive. Less commitment. Cash on the spot."

Aaron looks at Alexis, then back to me.

"That's so cool that that's your job."

"It's not really a job, but it's casual, so that's alright."

Alexis reaches out for my stick. I hand it to him and use the same motion to stand up to leave, wiping the sticky sugary residue on my shorts.

"A friend of mine has one underway," he tells me, standing a foot away. "She's probably looking for people it being near the end of the semester and not many students around. I can hook you up if you like?"

"What's involved?"

"It's just saying some words in a microphone."

"In front of people? No, that sounds awful."

"Not in front of people, ya dope, into a headset. It's so easy and pays a hundred bucks, on the spot, like you like. Wait here, I'll go see if I still have the info."

He's on mission in two strides. A bigger '13' glows on his back and disappears entirely after a right turn down the hall. Aaron's tending to a drip trailing down his forearm.

"I can't believe you lived with Lloyd Sumner. Did he squat you before bed? Did he make you make protein shakes? He got heaps of chicks, didn't he?"

I shake my head.

"Don't really know him to be honest. He mostly kept to himself."

Aaron looks disappointed.

"When he was fifteen, he had surgery to put steel rods in his toes because they were all curled up."

"Everyone knows that."

"He makes good lasagne," I offer. "That's all I've got,"

Alexis returns, standing in front of me about three times wider than me from this angle. He's holding out a white keycard. I take it from him and it gives nothing away. It's marked M-13 in black marker on one side, blank on the other.

"Now that I think about it, she did just have a baby, but it can't hurt to look. I've got class in twenty. I can show you where her office is if you want?"

"For real?"

"Yeah for real."

I'm not sure what he wants me to do with the keycard so I hand it back to him and ten minutes later, we're out the door.

USCRAY

For every one person who acknowledges Alexis with a wave or smile, two more take the perimetre on us. It could've been the face tattoo or just retaliation for the hostile glances I inadvertently offer passers-by on account of the steep incline we'd not yet accomplished. Sweat pits form, which doesn't help my mood.

"Can I push your bike for you?"

"No, I got it. Keep talking."

"What was I saying?"

"About Aaron's small stature."

"Oh right. So one day, me and Jarrad are playing Playstation, and Aaron— he's fourteen—comes home from school in tears. We'd never seen him cry, he's always so happy, so we think he's being bullied because he's pretty little and all. So me and D are rolling up our sleeves trying to find out who's doing it, then he tells us that after recess his teacher put on a documentary about sharks and how they're becoming extinct. Can you believe that?" He shakes his head.

"What's worse is we laughed at him. Imagine the damage that did? Anyway, the next day, I ate a fish burger and got so sick—like bright yellow bile sick—so since then the household has been vegetarian."

"How does that make him small?"

"Oh no, the two aren't related. I just still see him as that kid from that day. It's stuck with me. I guess it was the shock of seeing him crying about a thing like that. Then I wonder about the order of things. I don't know."

He looks down at me, then at my bike, then switches his bag from left to right shoulder.

"So me and Aaron are veg. Dynamite isn't, but he's cool with the principle of it so he's off meat at home. Problem is he doesn't like vegetables and he's lazy, so he only really eats cereal so his blood-sugar is whack making him prone to explosive mood swings and bad headaches, so he's extra moody. That was a snippet you saw back there. Worse now that he's got contract work. He's a teacher."

"Really? He looks so young."

"He's thirty-one."

"Seriously? He's aged well."

"Like an adequate cheese."

We cross the road and enter the campus. There's more people around than I would've expected for this time of night. Someone's smoking pot nearby.

"Anyway, I think that's why he spends so much time in his room, because he doesn't like exploding on people."

"It's nice that you've noticed that about him," I tell him. "So that's Jarrad, aka D?"

He nods once and smiles half.

"D—short for Dynamite, because of the mood swings."

"Ah, I see."

The campus looks particularly majestic this time of night. Buildings lit up in all the right places. Sheen and shadows stretch over the brick and gold glistens on the leaves moving to a cool breeze unavailable on ground level. Alexis switches his bag back to his left shoulder.

"Hey, I'm sorry to've put you on the spot back there, interrogating you about Sumner and asking what you do and all that. I hate when people do that."

I shrug.

"They're perfectly reasonable questions. I just don't really do anything and don't like explaining how little I do."

"I guess people don't know that going in though."

"I know."

"Why don't you prepare an answer that suits you? One that paints you exactly how you want to be seen and totally satisfies."

"I've tried that—doesn't work. People want to know why and what for and no answer ever satisfies. It's impossible."

"You need more conviction."

"I need any conviction."

He looks at me and smiles.

"So you care a lot what people think?"

"No."

His silence implies I find a more truthful answer. I concede.

"I care too much. I care about the all wrong things, and there are things I should care about but I can't seem to raise an iota of concern about. It's all out of whack."

"Well, what do you like to talk about?"

"Not myself."

"I didn't ask what you don't like to talk about."

Alexis tenses up but not because of my identity crisis. His eyes are locked on this girl with glowing red hair who's walking towards us. Her hair isn't glowing for any paranormal reason, simply because of the light above her head.

Ten silent paces build to an awkward reunion. The girl looks me up and down and Alexis forgets my name, so I point in the direction we were walking and continue on without saying a thing. A mirrored version of their conversation unfolds in the reflection of a window ahead of me.

Alexis is basically folded in half to match her level, but she's looking straight down to the concrete so her neck is exposed. He's holding his bag strap and smiling without showing teeth, trying to catch her eye, and for a moment it looks like he's going in for a kiss, but instead he rubs the top of her arm a few times. That was their farewell, then he's bridging the distance to meet me, looking at the pavement, white-knuckles wrapped around his bag strap. When he arrives, his eyes are a little glazed over.

"Girlfriend?"

"No, a friend." He moves his bag to his other shoulder and we walk the next ten metres in silence. The click of my chain chimes in every other paver or so.

"I am in love with her though."

He looks down at me and his pursed lips become a weak smile. He hitches his bag up because it falls when he tries to shrug off the matter.

"Does she know that?"

"No."

"Gonna tell her?"

"Nah, couldn't do it."

"Why not?"

"Because."

"Because why?"

"Because I'm gifted with foresight and burdened with crippling self-esteem issues when it comes to the ladies."

"Oh, is that all?"

He doesn't answer.

"Seems like she likes you."

"What makes you say that?"

"She laughed at your joke."

"What joke?"

"How you said today seemed more partly-cloudy than mostly-fine."

"Oh." He's dejected. All hope gone. "That wasn't a joke."

"Trust me, the way she doesn't look at you—she likes you."

"She likes me about as much as I like Dynamite which is about a medium. Here—" He over-rides my grip on the handlebars. "For the last leg, I'm doing it."

I feel like telling him he liked Dynamite more than a medium, and more than that I wanted to tell him to go for it with Red, but he put up two defenses already, so I don't press further.

"Thanks for taking me here," I say. "I appreciate the effort."

"It's no effort. It's on the way. Thanks for bringing the script."

"It was no effort, it was on the way."

He laughs one exhale laugh and looks up at the dated beige building which makes my hands feel dry just looking at it. It's cylindrical with more lights on than I would expect. Alexis manoeuvres my bike so the front wheel lands in an empty bike rack.

"This is the one. Do you have a lock for this relic?"

"I don't," I tell him. "I'm testing my faith in humanity."

"Risky business that. You might be walkin' home."

"You might be right."

"It's a long way."

I shrug.

"Okay weirdo. She's on the sixth floor. M-13. Her name is Rachel. From memory it's a right out the lift, but like I said, she might not be there now, but you can try your luck. I know she was nocturnal pre-baby, but hey, at least now you know where to go. I'd be keen to know if she remembers me."

"I'll drop your name."

"Alexis," he points to his chest.

"Louise," I point to mine.

He shifts his backpack again and nods a nod goodbye, heading back where we came from.

There's something in the way he walks; a grace to his step. Soft edges, no angst. Strange as it sounds, his movement makes me sure he'll end up with the red-headed girl eventually, it's just a matter of time and space.

AURORA

A welcome side-effect of the sleep experiment is improved night vision. It's heightened accuracy mixed with the serenity available pre-dawn creates this dream-like effect where my four shadows are companion enough and the silence stifles the onslaught of thoughts—to an extent, anyway. The only downside to the hour are the repeated headlines driveway after driveway.

SAFETY NIGHTMARE

SAFETY NIGHTMARE

SAFETY NIGHTMARE

In every driveway there's a SAFETY NIGHTMARE.

The newspaper honchos have tuned into the fact that the footpaths hold damp after the midnight downpour so they've made contingency measures to enclose the papers in plastic to ensure the sentiment isn't lost.

Once, on 'Girl Bludgeoned With Her Own Stiletto' day, I filled my basket with as many papers that would fit so at least those households might've enjoyed their morning beverage in peace, but then I had to throw them all away and that didn't sit right either. Current day, in lieu of thievery, I spend my time riding with my eyes to the sky, or challenging myself by reading very small lettering on dimmed out signs very far away.

My journey begins on this secret bike path not so secret for anyone who travels south down the Birchmore hill long enough to find the well-worn arrow pointing to a metre-wide opening between a laundromat and a dilapidated cigarette factory. After about a hundred metres of over-grown vines and dirt terrain, it opens to a path running parallel to the train line taking said cyclist to the canal in half the effort of the mainstream commute.

The decline takes care of the next kilometre, leading to a six lane highway which can be crossed with eyes closed and a trained ear at this hour. Under a bridge decorated with a blue and green owl saying *Release*, then it's a short 'Z' route followed by vacant old shopfronts with upside down light-boxes and newspaper covering the windows.

The east to west streets house the ancient bodegas and the north to south streets are mostly residential, similar to the walk-ups in our neighbourhood but made with a lower quality mortar. If one rides down any one of the back-alleys where residents access their driveways, glimpses of backyards flash through the wooden fence slats like an old cartoon with only a few slides per scene. Some yards are up-kept, made for entertaining with polished decks and umbrellas and ferns pot-ted nearby. Some are made up of plastic chairs, faded kids playgrounds and expired paint tins. Others have improved their fencing situation, and the contents of their yards remain a mystery.

When the road changes from smooth to cobblestone, I take to the footpath with enough momentum behind me to end up on the ramp above the bench seat where the drunk Swede usually sits.

I've met this guy twice and seen him four times in total. Once I got to him when he'd just opened his brown paper bottle and we had a chat about how he couldn't help which vaginal canal he came from and to judge anyone about that detail is ludicrous. He told me he didn't pick his and couldn't change it even if he wanted to, so the point is moot and there are better things to argue about. The next time he couldn't coerce any more liquid from the bottle so we sat in silence. The third time he was in an argument when I arrived—with himself—and I didn't want to get in the middle of that, so I watched him from the pier balcony while the sun rose behind me. The fourth time he was swearing at pigeons and throwing coins into the canal, and I knew enough about him by then to keep my distance.

Today, there's only the empty paper bottle and some guy operating one of those gutter clearing vehicles on the road above and behind, so I sit with the empty bottle at my feet, turn off my night vision and concentrate on the horizon, willing it to open up. I imagine this vapour leaking in, bright lights resembling the Aurora Borealis—coloured and gaseous and evolving. It'd hover over the water, lingering there for long enough to convince me of its existence. I'd pinch myself to make sure I wasn't dreaming, then look around to see if anyone else bore witness. The gutter cleaner would confirm the sighting with nod of acknowledgement, and once we both had the proof we needed, we'd look back and the vapour would sink to the bottom the canal, then this satisfying catharsis would overcome us, and we'd come out lighter, without the tar between muscle fibres. Then we'd float up the hill, no effort at all.

RENEGADE

It takes me ages to realise what this girl is doing. At first I thought she might've lost something the way she's looking around the dirt like that, lifting her knees for all they're worth to navigate over roots, slapping bark as she goes.

It's on her third appearance on the southwest side of the ancient truck that I notice the pile of chains not ten steps away from her, and it's then I understand that this isn't a meagre case of a lost charm bracelet or missing Little Mermaid figurine—this girl is on a mission.

Being a Wednesday and the good side of ten, no-one else on the mountain's skirt seems to notice this —maybe eleven—year old girl tugging the end of an indeterminable length of chain with all her might.

No parental figures in sight.

No guardians of any kind.

With every rotation her furrow intensifies. She makes it four laps around the tree with some surplus chain left over. After an extra lap to inspect her work, she stops on northwest side, completely out of sight.

Although it appears she's trying to *save* the tree, she doesn't realise it but she's cutting fat chunks of bark out at her six o'clock.

Curious about her mission, I approach carefully and from an angle.

"Cool chains," I say. "Where'd you get them?"

The girl is nestled deep in the roots like they've grown around her, so much so, she doesn't hear my question. She's contained by the chains sitting bolt upright against the trunk. I step closer and repeat myself. Her response is a wary and reluctant expression.

"They look brand new," I add, inspecting the silver links with faux interest.

"That's because they are."

"It must've been heavy going getting them up all those steps?"

"Wasn't that hard."

With excellent dexterity she inserts a padlock between two links, closes it, then turns the combination wheel a bunch of times in both directions. She then collects the residual chain to make a small silver pile underneath her crossed legs, sits up a little taller then deflates back down.

"Is this about that big orange X?"

"Of course it is," her eyes pierce mine. "They're going to chop it down."

Her words—fueled with passion and duty—vibrate up beyond the peak of the canopy to rattle the flagpoles at the look-out, then they fall back down to earth, settling in the space in my body where passion and duty might one day reside.

It goes left eye, right eye, left eye, right and the tree behind her falls away and the green around me falls away and her freckles exist on a canvas of pure white for a noteable stretch of time. She then drops her head and looks at her palms.

I didn't particularly feel like hugging a tree, but it was nice to know it was an option.

"You know I think it's going to rain soon. Looks pretty bleak out."

She shrugs once, heavy. "It's just water."

"That's true," I agree, amused and in awe. "So, do you want me to call the police to get you started, or are you going to do this the old fashioned way?"

"Old fashioned way. Now go away please."

RACHEL

I'm up three flights of stairs before it dawns on me that I have no idea where I'm going. Few details of Alexis' directions remain, and the room numbers don't correspond, so when I get to the sixth, I knock until someone responds to Rachel. I find her four doors in and it appears she's been expecting me. Before I can offer any introduction, she waves me into her office and instructs me to sit in the chair opposite her desk, then holds up her finger, as if to pause me while she reads something the screen infront of her.

"One sec. I just need to finish this paragraph."

I sit as instructed and study this woman. She doesn't look at all like I imagined. I thought she'd be slender and tall with gingery-blonde hair and a serious face, but in reality, she's my build with thick dark hair collected with at least ten bobby pins atop a round, friendly, mum-like face, shielded by brown rimmed glasses. She's backlit by the window above her which illuminates an extra inch of curls glowing copper around her head. In her right hand is a red mug, contents unknown. She's got a tea stain high on her shirt.

The office is busy, hectic, overwhelming. Action across all surfaces. Piles of books and papers and folders. Towers of cardboard filing boxes stacked around the place. Nine boxes—three by three—are pushed up against the wall beneath her framed academic achievements.

Rachel shifts in her chair and looks between Post-it note stuck to the edge of her screen, then to the screen, then to the Post-it note, and then she rolls to the far end of her L-shaped desk, grabs a white mug from the shelf and fills it from the ceramic water well. She offers me the mug and I take a sip as she reaches for a manila folder marked PSOS 2-12.

"So, it's Sarah, right? Thanks for coming. Are you're a student here?"

"No, I'm not," I tell her, choking water down the wrong pipe. "And my name's not Sarah either."

Rachel studies my seriousness over her glasses. Tiny reflections of the lights overhead glint in both lens. The folder is halfway open and whether it will open completely remains to be seen. She looks confused.

"You're not here for the speech perception experiment?"

"I am, but I'm not Sarah. She must've got caught up. I know Alexis. He mentioned you might be looking for participants. My name is Louise. Louise Beckman."

Rachel considers the information and responds with a single nod, then looks at the bottom right side of her screen. If that clock says the same as the one on the filing cabinet behind her, it reads ten seconds to twelve fifteen.

Her forehead creases. Lips purse in contemplation.

"Alright then, let's go with this."

The folder opens and flattens against the desk. The contents are made up of half crumpled sheets, half fresh ones. Rachel moves her glasses down her nose.

"So Louise, is this your first time as a research participant?"

"No."

"Have you read the outline of the study?"

"No. I have no idea what's about to happen."

From the bottom of the fresh stack she slides out a form about six pages thick and stapled in the corner. She puts it next to my now empty mug.

"All the details you need are on the front page. Then it's a matter of ticking a few boxes, writing a few sentences and we'll go from there."

"We're doing it now? I just thought I'd see if I could make an appointment."

"Well, since your here... does that work for you?"

I weigh up my options and prior commitments and confirm there aren't any. I nod and she nods too, then she swipes her lanyard and keys from the bowl next to her computer and stands so she's twice as tall as me from this angle.

"Use as much detail as you can and if anything doesn't make sense, leave it blank. I'll go prep the lab, be back in ten. Any questions before I go?"

I silently tell her I have many, but she's got this closed lip smile happening and is basically already in transit, so I shake my head and she leaves the room. The click of her heels echo in sync with the second hand. Twelve steps later, it's just the clock.

Stand-out words on the front page include repetition, response, clarity, perception and compensation. Basic information is required on the next page: name, date of birth, student status, emergency contact, medical history and so on, and the following pages involve Likert scales and physiological ratings. The last three pages are qualitative; two questions on each page.

It's been three minutes since Rachel left the room and the completed questionnaires lie dormant, beckoning my inquiry. Everything else in the office blurs into the background, which begs the question that perhaps this speech experiment is a placebo for a more detailed experiment involving privacy and a hidden camera.

Four seconds pass I feel prepared to face the consequences. Being ultra careful—which means without breath—I remove the first questionnaire.

Name: Daniel Armcoe

Age: 22

Student: ☑ ☐N

3. Family medical history (please tick)

Cancer	☑	Depression	☑	Leukemia	☐	Epilepsy	☑
Heart Disease	☑	Bi-Polar	☐	Thyroid disease	☐	Hepatitis A	☐
Diabetes	☐	Asthma	☐	Stroke	☐	Hepatits B or C	☐
Alzheimers	☐	Chest pains	☐	Glaucoma	☐	Convulsions	☐

5. Please mark how you generally feel during social situations

	Always	Most Of The Time	Sometimes	Never
Nervous			X	
Confident				X
Anxious		X		
Relaxed			X	

6. Amount of close friends (that you see more than 3 x per month)

1-3 ⟨3-5⟩ 5-8 8+

9. What social situations affect your physiological state most noticeably?

Public speaking

10. Do you think it's getting better or worse?

No different. Probably because I'm not do-ing anything different

11. Are there any recurring anxieties in your day to day that you've recognised as particularly exhaustive? (leave blank if none)

12. Any significant situations in the last six months which have sparked feelings of anxiety and/or loss of control? (leave blank if none)

Footsteps echo on the off-beat just as I'm replacing Daniel's questionnaire in its position on top of the pile, when I notice the second one down.

Name: *OWEN FLETCHER*

Age: *25*

Student : ✓ ☐

The door clicks open at three seconds to twelve twenty-five. Rachel makes her way behind her desk, assertive in her stride and grabbing exactly the papers she needs at the exact moment she walks by. She creates a breeze which reminds me to take a long overdue breath.

The folder is wide open and I can't tell if she's noticed it's not quite how she left it. She looks as though she's just washed her face.

"Okay. Let's see where you're at." She sits down and holds out her hand. Her tone suggests she's none-the-wiser about my actions, though she could just be well practiced. I offer her my pages and in lieu of watching her face for signs of disappointment, I take stock of the details of her office while she flips through my questionnaire.

After removing all things professionally related, four things seem brighter against the beige: a photo of a newborn baby with a squished red face, a bottle painted with blackboard paint, a pink love heart sticker at the top left corner of her phone, and on the window sill; a plant with dangling heart-shaped leaves only reachable if she was standing on the filing cabinet, and say, maybe, four of those thick books.

"So, none of it made sense?" The form loses its gusto in her hand, curving over like a breaking wave, much like the impression she must've had about me.

"Hmm?"

"You didn't fill out any of the questions... "

"I know. Sorry about that. I'm not sure this is the right place... Alexis said this involved talking into a microphone?"

Rachel's swivelling in her seat, likely contemplating whether I'm dyslexic or illiterate or both. I completely understand her confusion since Daniel, Owen and a whole stack of other people were able to fill out their forms in the ten minute time allotted.

"The experiment has morphed since Alexis was here, in fact, it's morphed a few times since then. That was a few semesters ago now."

"Right. Well, could you explain the aim of the study? I skimmed the first page but couldn't really grasp the premise."

"Unfortunately Louise, I can't really give out too many more details than what you read because it could affect the data you provide, but there'll be a full debrief after, so if you're happy to continue, we can."

She stops swivelling to wait for my answer. I nod, then she picks up her pen.

"Alright, so, not a student?"

"No."

"Phone number?"

"Not applicable. My phone got run over a few months ago."

"So no phone?"

"No."

"Okay...what about emergency contact?"

I tell her my parent's details even though they were redundant details, then go on to tell her my address, my birthday and we move on to the scales where I rate how I feel in the moment. Part of me wants to tell her the data wouldn't be relevant by the end of the experiment let alone the end of this exchange, but I don't want to add to the confusion of her already see-sawing vision.

With every question we cover, the clouds move quickly behind the plant erasing the question prior. Sometimes glimpses of blue sky show, but it's mostly dark greys that turn to neon green depending on my depth perception. I'm thinking about the girl on the skirt of the mountain, wondering if she's still chained up when the last syllable of my name rebounds around the room. Rachels's wide-eyed, waiting for an answer to a question I haven't heard.

"Are you still here? Have you gone somewhere else?"

"Sorry, I got distracted. A bird flew by. It looked like it was on fire. Could you repeat the question?"

She puts her hands flat against the desk and looks at me over her glasses so her forehead wrinkles up.

"Any recurring anxieties? If so, please provide an example."

Recurring anxieties?

Where to begin..

"Well, the other day I rode all the way to Westwood and as soon as I got there I rode straight home because I felt sure I left the oven on."

She pens in my answer.

"And did you?"

"Did I leave the oven on?"

She nods.

"No, I didn't."

"Okay. Any significant incidents in the last six months, Louise? Something unexpected that has shaken your regular patterns? Thrown you through a loop?"

The space between us fills with all the possible answers.

"No, none that I can think of."

"Could you try? The question's half the page."

"Sorry, nothing significant."

Rachel studies me carefully and we say something silently to each other. I'm not sure what she said to me, but I apologise sincerely and ask her how will we go on from here.

She puts her pen down and props her elbows on the armrests, clasping her fingers together. Her breath is measured and she doesn't look impressed. She's been so patient so far I feel obliged to offer her something of substance.

"Have you ever seen Men in Black?" I ask her. "The first one?"

She nods a single downward nod. "I think so."

"That part, where the guy's face opens up, and there's this little alien sitting in his head at the helm of this whole control panel? I think that's what's going on here."

After four strikes of the second hand, she pulls herself into her desk and picks up her pen.

"Are you the alien or the guy?"

"I'm both."

"And do you think it's getting better or worse?"

"No different. Probably because I'm not doing anything different."

Whether she's writing that or something else I can't tell from this angle.

"Usually I'm fine," I explain. "But then I leave the house or have a conversation with someone and it all starts unravelling."

She flicks back over the first two pages.

"Are you really fine, usually?" she asks, absently.

"Sorry?"

"You said, *usually I'm fine*. I'm wondering what your standard of fine is?"

My standard of fine?

Regular.

Medium.

Normal.

"Any drug use in the last six months Louise?"

"No. No drugs."

She crosses out a section on the front page and slides her glasses on top of her head so there's no shield between us.

"Okay, that'll do for now. Let's head up to the lab."

THE LAB

It's pitch black until the screen goes on. Three beeps later the word 'HID' flashes in white for one count, then disappears. My duty is to say the word that appears on the screen into this microphone headset similar to the kind used by a fighter pilot or office receptionist. It would continue like that—HID, HEAD, HID, HEAD—for four rounds of three minutes. Between each round is a minute break.

Rachel said she'd check on me at every break which seemed excessive, but I soon understood why. In addition to the vocal cord constriction, it didn't take long before I felt the onset of a massive freakout brewing. About halfway through the first round, the difference between the words evaporated completely, which is about the point where I feel like I'm about to implode. My head itches fire ants, the seat offers little in the way of support and this pulse in my joints beckons for fast motion out of this tiny room and away from this environment. I react before prompted and then it doesn't even feel like I'm saying words anymore—just noises. I'm slurring my responses, and eventually it doesn't even feel like they're coming from me. Accuracy turns sloppy. Time bends around letters.

If Rachel decided to ask those multiple choice questions again, I'd probably rate anxiety at a ten, claustrophobia at a ten, and overwhelm at a ten plus.

HEAD

HID

HEAD

HID

HID

HID

HEAD

HID

It goes on like that incessantly until finally the door swings open. The sudden shift prompts a cluster of manic white spots to gravitate between us. Rachel's smiling like she understands my duress.

"Are you ok?"

I nod a few small nods because I'm sure my *yes* would come out a slur.

"You've got about three minutes and you're done."

Time is relative, I swear.

I feel much better upon exiting the tiny black room. Even more so as we cross through the transit zone between wings and I realise we're a corridor away from compensation. Rachel's a few steps ahead. She looks back for an answer to another question I haven't heard, so I nod once and smile half which seems to satisfy her. Twelve steps and one turn later, she's pressing her keycard against the panel by the door, then she's pulling herself into her desk. I figure it's as good an opportunity as any.

"Rachel, can I asked you a question?"

She's reaching to slide open a drawer which I suspect holds the petty cash tin. Her silence says *go on*.

"What are your qualifications?"

No petty cash comes out of the drawer, only the PSOH folder. My form goes on top and the folder goes back in the drawer.

"Ph.D. in behavioural psychology. The rest you can see for yourself."

She motions to the wall.

"Okay. That wasn't my question, more of a precursor."

"Fire away."

"Before, when you asked me, *are you still here? Have you gone somewhere else?* Well, that's exactly it."

"Go on."

"I guess I have this... underlying dissatisfaction, which really isn't underlying at all really, it's prevalent on all levels, and believe me, I am aware that even saying this paints me as extremely ungrateful, which compounds the problem, but underneath it all I have this sense of..."

Rachel's eyebrows ascend inviting me to go on but I can't encourage the next string of words together. An image of the girl in chains gets caught up in the mix, raindrops hit the window like their aiming straight at me.

"Sense of what Louise?"

"It's just that I'm... I'm going about my days, not doing anything of consequence, but I'm seeing all these incredible, beautiful things; these really stunning forces of nature that a lot of people seem oblivious to—which is fine—because it's like it's meant just for me and I love that—but it feels so... fleeting, and when I tune back in to everyone, and I'm watching them go about their lives, moving with this hurried purpose and making up excuses that you know are excuses, but somehow, it's all acceptable, necessary, needed even, and I feel so... removed, from all of it, like I'm on another plain, looking in."

It's not until the echo of my words evaporate that I register I've been looking everywhere in the office except at her. Rachel's dead still. The only movement she makes is to furrow her eyebrows further. Eventually she starts flicking a pen between her fingers.

"I hear now how you might've heard that and I think I've misrepresented myself. That happens alot when I speak. I may be indolent, but I'm not depressed."

"A little indolence every now and then is necessary to take stock of things, don't you think?"

"Maybe. But maybe I've just got too much time on my hands and I'm thinking my way down a funnel."

"What are your main concerns then, aside from the excuses?"

"It's this... unspoken influence. I don't know how explain it, but there's also this inevitable spoken one coming at me at every turn; people telling me to think this way, try this method, decide what I want, stand in my truth, then others are telling me to think less and that I shouldn't rely on my thoughts, that I should put credence in my feelings, but my feelings are as fleeting as my thoughts, so finding any stable grounds for rationale is impossible."

At first it looks like I've deeply offended her, but then she lets out this laugh. I can't believe it. It's clear she didn't mean too, it just... erupted out of her so we're left gaping at each other. I guess my expression tells her it's not really a laughing matter. Rachel shifts upright.

"Well, there's something there. Have you asked yourself what you want?"

"I want to be rid of these handlebar shoulders, for starters. This feeling of constriction and obligation all through me. It's like I'm gripping my handlebars so tight even when I'm nowhere near my bike. It's at its worst when I think about getting a job or attending social engagements, the normal things people my age do—which tells me one thing."

"What's that?"

"That proceeding in that direction can only be detrimental if I'm already reacting so adversely to the thought of it."

She tries to conceal it, but I can tell she's concerned. I figure this is the first and only time I'll see her so I cut my losses and decide to pile it on.

"Also, I'm causing significant damage to the house."

"To your house?"

"Yeah. I've broken the laundry doors. I pulled the tap out of the wall. I made the fly-screen fall off."

"Are you sure that's you? They sound like common faults from years of use."

"No, it's my force. I'm tense all the time."

She looks around her office likely searching for a diagnosis.

"Well, we could look in one of these books and find some term to define you, but nouns become pretty useless after a point, don't you think?"

"Nouns are useless?"

"What I mean is, they only get you so far."

Rachel centres herself in line with me, pulls herself in and two ticks later she's taking off her glasses. She fold them up and shifts some papers into a stack.

"Louise, have you ever heard of the Hundredth Monkey Effect?"

"Is that me? I'm the hundredth monkey?"

She laughs a subtler laugh which diffuses the concern at the corners of her eyes. She shakes her head and tilts it compassionately.

"No, it's this idea that sometimes, you don't see anything changing from where you're standing, but all it takes is this one little thing that looks like nothing, or it might look like something, and then everything starts changing radically."

"Okay, well, how long does it take for this hundredth monkey to get his act together?"

She rests back into her chair and clasps her hands together.

"How long is a piece of string?"

"Ugh, my dad says that all the time."

It goes left eye, right eye, left eye, right.

"More often than not we don't notice what our efforts yield instantaneously, and there's usually a good reason for it."

"So you're telling me to be patient and wait for some big or small cue I may or may not see?"

She nods once. Then picks up her glasses and slides them into a case. The case slides into her handbag and she collects her personals again, then zips her bag shut to indicate the question segment of the afternoon had come to an end.

"Since you've got some time on your hands, spend some time over the next two weeks in a place you feel good, where you can relax—no pressure. I'll have a better answer for you next session."

"Next session? I thought that was it?"

"No." She looks concerned for my well-being again. "I mentioned this upstairs."

"Oh, must've missed that."

Rachel's on her feet, bag on her shoulder.

"Next session—in two weeks—we repeat this task, from there we'll schedule a third session followed by a brief interview. The whole thing shouldn't take longer than two hours all up, it's segmented which is a pain in the ass, but, it's necessary. Same time in a fortnight okay? I'll scrub out Sarah and pencil you in. And I'll have the first half of the payment for you too."

That much commitment really did well to spike my anxiety, which felt ironic and maybe intentional, but I find myself nodding anyway.

"Have you got a place in mind?"

"A place for what?"

"To relax?"

"I don't know how to relax."

Rachel waits for me to compose a better answer.

"I have one idea." I tell her.

She nods once.

"Okay good. And if it's quick cash you're after, head to the Walsh-Bennett lab. There's an audio sensory experiment underway that runs in the night and pays there and then."

CELESTIAL

There isn't a flicker of energy, human or otherwise. Rustling elephant ears tell me the residents don't mind my presence and I have to agree with them based on the observations I'd made so far. Those observations being that no-one's called the authorities or notified the obese gentleman who sits in the glass cube by the boom-gate. His role is about as useful to the residents as our super is to us.

Being the only security member on duty this time of night, from where I lurked, it felt important to tell him that having his head and upper torso consumed almost entirely by the newspaper made him easy to bypass and rendered him use-less. If the implication didn't lead to my incrimination, I might've made the effort.

The pond in the middle of the establishment is glassy and calm. Reflection: perfecto. Other than my footsteps and the occasional rogue pebble, the only sound comes from the belting of the electricity box, also known as — my boost to paradise.

It's usual hum and moan ceases the moment I step on it, starting up again as I turn over the stone wall topped with terracotta roof tiles which scrape against my shorts and remind me how thirsty I am.

Burnt palm tips graze on my descent — the perfect amount to stifle my land-ing, however, the triumph of another smooth entry dissipates like blown ash as soon as I see I'm not the only late night pool goer at New Heights Retirement Village.

Paralysis overwhelms, bringing this old guy ten times closer and everything else ten times further away.

He's ninety-two—at least—and despite the hour, he's wearing dark glasses as big as safety goggles. He's decked out in the kind of shorts they used to wear in professional tennis back in the day when the get-up was all white and tight. He's almost on a full recline. Skin is tissue-paper thin, especially around his ribs here his hands are clasped over the apex like they're strapping him in. Over his stomach is this white scar, glimmering like a snail's trail, about two feet long reaching up to his armpit. It's lit up by the moon. His bony feet pointing to the stars.

A waft of night jasmine blows by at nose level, and somewhere in the confusion, I've taken to a half-squat position amongst the yuccas by the drinking fountain, completely at odds about what to do next. My heartbeat sends ripples to the other end of the pond and bugs I'd never find vibrate a sound that I imagine lactic acid build-up would sound like.

In my efforts to disembark from the squat, a wayward and tremendously useless garden light meets the full force of what would be my first step away. I fall sideways; hip scrapes the base of a palm, knees are pierced by wood chips beneath. The lactic acid bugs scream warnings of an intruder.

Moongoggles hasn't moved an inch. His glasses must've blinded him to the point he could no longer hear. His feet are perfectly still. Foliage moves breezily around him.

If he could hear, I figure he might've mistaken me for a large inept cat, however, I'm told otherwise when his hand lifts like a marionette, tapping the neighbouring moon-chair twice, then resuming clasped position over his scar trail.

I feel like I have little choice in the matter and since his reaction is calm so far, I approach, anticipating a warning about trespassing which was probably something I needed to hear.

The moon-chair creaks as I sit. Nothing about him changes. He doesn't turn his head, just keeps it angled towards the tips of the palms above the electricity box. Eyes closed, eyes open—I don't know. If he could see through those glasses he would've witnessed the invasion inch for inch.

Movement is concentrated in his chest. Up and down to the rhythm of his shallow breaths. He seems peaceful though, like airing any sounds of apology would disrupt his serenity.

I'll wait for him to speak first—that's respectful.

On my way to a full recline, the moon shines off his right lens like he's winking at me. We lie there silently listening to bugs, watching burnt palm tips graze while I mentally will him to tell me the story about who left that scar on his chest.

BELUGA

Usually Thursdays at the home-state means a vacant house, at least until after dark, so finding Selby standing in front of the freezer tracing the cool vapour with her eyelids comes as a surprise. Her hair's pulled back with a t-shirt wrap so she's got accidental quiffs all over and she's balancing a bag of frozen edamame on each shoulder. One falls to the floor when my entrance excites the houses' arthritis and the other falls when she turns to inspect the intruder.

"Oh good, it's you." She kneels down next to retrieve both bags. "Do you know anything about the half watermelon in the freezer?"

"I can't explain it." I tell her, rifling through the basket on the microwave in search of my house key.

"If you're looking for answers, you won't find them there."

She hands me one of the packets. It's wonderfully cold. She pushes a hole in her packet to extract a pod.

"Have you seen my key?" I ask her. "It's nowhere in the world."

"Oh, was that you knocking on my window last night? Sorry Lou, I thought it was Gustave."

"Cat's don't knock, Sel."

"Gustave understands French. He can do anything."

I give up my search and pull out a chair at the kitchen table. It scrapes along the floor annoying a bird on the balcony, so much so, he flies away.

No action underway at The Dope Haus. No progress on their fort.

"Sorry Lou, haven't seen it, but I'm not doing anything for the rest of the day if you're heading to work, so you don't have to worry about locking the door. I'll leave mine under the barbeque if I go out."

Selby sits opposite me and starts a pile of empty pod shells between us. It seems like a good as time as any.

"Sel, I haven't had a job for over five months."

Her inital reaction is stillness then suspicion, then she silently pieces evidence together as she chews. I defer my attention to my edamame packet, smoothing it out across my lap to allow equal distribution of pods and chill.

"That makes a lot of sense actually."

She pulls the string off another pod.

"How does that make sense?"

"Zac keeps mentioning he's seeing you around the place when you say you're at work."

"I never *say* I'm at work—it's assumed."

"A play on rhetoric—classic Lou." She adds another empty pod to the pile. "So what happened? Did you get fired?"

"Sort of."

"What do you mean sort of?"

"They stopped giving me shifts."

"How come?"

"Because I stopped going. They might still be giving me shifts, I don't know."

She tilts her head speculatively, then sits alert and upright indicating she's ready for all the information. I slide a pile of A4 papers towards me from the stack next to the fruit bowl for something room-temperature to fiddle with.

Her silence is the question and she keeps asking over and over again.

"Do we have to? It's really, very boring."

"Yes, we do—five months later."

"I don't know Sel. All of a sudden it seemed so... unimportant."

"What happened though?"

"I don't know... I was driving to work one day, but didn't turn to go in, I just kept driving. One block, many blocks. Six hours later I'm in some small town called Newton and it's getting dark so I put a for sale sign up in the back window of the Honda and when I wake up, some guy's standing by the passenger door calling me about it. An hour later I'm on the bus back home, and since then, not much."

"You got a bike."

"Yes, I got a bike."

She studies the inside of a pod.

"So how are you paying rent then? With the car money?"

"Yeah."

"Cool. I wish I could do that."

"You can do it. Although, I must say it's not quite the new lease on life I was hoping for. I'm more tense than ever. Doesn't make sense."

"Probably because you have a finite amount of financial security."

"I'm sure that's part of it."

"So what do you do all day then?"

"Bike around, look for signs."

"Found any?"

"No stopping, there's a lot of those."

She looks unimpressed.

"These birds are talking to me, telling me things."

"And what about the project?"

"What project?"

"Zac said you were doing some research thing. He said that you were super vague about it and he didn't believe you were really involved in such a thing."

"Did he now?"

"He did."

Another empty pod on the pile.

"Well?"

"That's just what I say when I need a placeholder for my day of not much."

"Wouldn't it be easier to say you're not doing anything?"

"No. People don't react well to that. Their heads jerk back and float around and then they look at their hands or off into the distance. They want to know why and how and what for and no answer is ever good enough."

She looks up at me, wide-eyed, like she's solved it.

"Oh hey, this is perfect then—can you be here next Tuesday around nine? Allan's coming to fix the laundry door."

"Do you mean next Tuesday, or three Wednesdays from now when he remembers the appointment?"

"It's really hard to say."

"I will if you answer me one question?"

"No. No way. Okay what?"

"What's this?" I hold up the page I'm fiddling with. In the top right corner is a crest with *Waesly Academy Studio Scholarship application* written underneath. Apparently Selby is also having some trouble finding the answers to some very basic questions. Her shoulders fall, then she looks real mad, discards her pod and wipes her reaction away with both hands, morphing her face into the only arrangement where she could look un-pretty.

"I can't talk about that today Lou, I can't."

"No-one can draw maps like you Sel."

She's shaking her head.

"Nope. Sorry. Can't do it today. This week I'm on holidays, I absolutely am. And in light of not-so-recent developments, I think you should join me—starting with a pool visit. I'm melting Lou, I really think I'm melting."

⊘

It's like we've been transplanted from the kitchen to the 12m mark of Birchmore pool with the mechanism from that old Skilltester game. Neil's floral cap skims along in lane four, the kid isn't working and the boss isn't around either, just more bronzed men shaped like Neil; pot-bellied and thin-legged. Parents with infant kids buzz around and a few gay guys lay towel-top near ours. It's strategic placement on our part, to keep ourselves safe from infiltration.

Bodies splash, kids run, squeal, jump, gasp, laugh while bees hover just above the surface as if proximity alone is cooling enough. Behind my eyelids neon shapes morph in the dark; sunsets of red and orange with occasional bolts of green depending on squint pressure. The shapes tune in nicely with the leisure racket.

"How long do I have to look to the heavens before I have an epiphany?" Selby asks. Her arms are stretched wide over the lane ropes and her head's tipped back so the bottom half of her curls are straight and wet.

"What are you trying to epiph?"

She rolls over to face the open section of the pool, resting her chin on the bulbs.

"How to live free like they did in the nineties, when everybody was naturally radiant and vibrant and saving each others lives while wearing resort wear and singing when they felt like it."

From where I'm positioned it looks like she's watching this girl splashing about two lanes over. Her hair is so blonde she looks bald and she's only got one front tooth. She isn't at all concerned about the aestetic variance.

A blurry group of school kids hop and jump their way to the wading pool. Heatwave residue contained in the concrete has them dancing to avoid foot-singe.

"Everything seemed so much simpler then. Remember Baywatch?"

"Do you think it was simpler because you were six or because of the half-hour concentration of drama?"

"Probably because I was six."

"Why are these children still in school? I don't understand it."

"It's out of hours care. Fuck Lou Lou."

"What?"

"My hair's stuck."

Upon inspection I note a wet chunk of her hair has knotted between two bulbs. I move nearer to help and in her struggle for freedom, she punches me dead in the left eye.

"Fuck, I'm so sorry Lou."

"*Keep* still for a second," I tell her.

I inspect the damage with my one good eye, the other is filled with either pool water or tears. Selby submits to a float, squinting skyward with jewels in her lashes.

"What's going on?" I ask her.

"I don't know. A lot of things really, but right now I'm thinking about Zac."

"What about him?"

"We're just so tense lately."

"Oh? I hadn't noticed."

"That's because you're never home."

"Touché."

She growls and rubs her right eye. "It's like whenever we see each other we're walking into a dual—swords above heads, ready to strike." She squints up at me. "Do you know how heavy a sword is Lou? So heavy. It's exhausting."

"Well, what's causing it?"

"I don't know. Last night I tried talking to him about it. He goes, *nut—fuck that, don't want to have this conversation.* Which is fair enough too, cause I don't want to have it either, but lately, I'm asking myself what I even get from it. We stated our intent way back when and it doesn't fit anymore and now it looks like we can't revise it."

"Just revise it, say the opposite thing."

"I tried. Believe me, I've tried."

"So what are you going to do?"

"I've been thinking about it, how to make it better, and I'll reach this conclusion that feels good and I'll be having a great day, then he comes home all amped up from his shit day and it bounds onto me so I forget the conclusion and we have this crap encounter, then it's night time and he's asleep and I'll remember that Zen state I thought I found and be like, *oh, why didn't I apply that? That could've all gone ten times smoother.* It's like I always remember who I want to be about ten minutes before I fall asleep."

She splashes her face in an effort to erase the problem and I find release for her hair. After clearing a careful distance to avoid more bulb trouble, she dips her head back to eradicate all curls.

"I'm not really sure what to tell you, Sel."

"Don't put too much stock in what I'm saying today, I'm having a moment this week. I just need to vent here so I don't let it out on him."

She swims toward me.

"On a brighter note I spoke to your dad before. He said to say he's in Cambodia. He said your mum's loving it and they're staying with a family of fourteen nursing a baby elephant back to life. Her name is Ruby and they found her on the side of the road on the way back from the airport. He said you shouldn't worry, and he'll call again soon."

"Cambodia?"

"Yeah, can you believe it?"

"I'd say I can't, but there are more witnesses to the contrary. Fourteen of them, apparently."

Selby's watching the little bald blonde girl coughing up chlorine poolside, probably thinking about Baywatch.

"Do you want to come to Belvedere tonight?" she asks. "A few people from the show are going. It should be fun."

"Nah, not tonight."

"Big plans?"

"Yep."

"Maybe doing something social and conformist would be good for you. It might be exactly the situation you need. "

"No, that wouldn't help me. I know it definitely wouldn't help me."

Selby withholds her comment because she knows the subject is closed. Instead she floats on her back so her ears are underwater.

Neil turns at the north end. Teen Lifeguard arrives. He's rubbing his eyes like the sun's offending him.

"Did you say something?" Selby asks, surfacing.

"I asked you when are you going to fill out that form?"

She squints my way then takes the easy way out, going where there are no questions and no answers. Five metres later she resurfaces; water falls off her and she looks like a girl of six again.

"No, see Lou, it's harder with that one because... I care the most about it."

She launches backwards kicking splashes in my face.

"If you care the most about it shouldn't it take up most of your time?"

Her laugh is cut off when she dips under the lane ropes into Neil's lane. When she resurfaces this time she pretends to put on goggles.

"If I lived in that much a ratio of self doubt I'd feel a lot worse than that little girl just did. I'm going to see if I can complete a lap." And off she goes.

With as much air I can gather, I follow her under. Fifteen counts before the first bubble, and I hold for ten more, closing my eyes so tight the colours emerge and I can almost hear what Neil is thinking. From here it sounds something like, *you've got a long way to go before you'll be swimming with the belugas, love.*

WALSH-BENNETT #1

No-one knows what I'm talking about when I ask about the audio sensory experiment that runs in the night and pays there and then. Mostly because only cleaners are around at this hour and it's not their job to know these things. The notice boards bear no reference to it and the information desk has no man behind it. Every floor is completely vacant and I'm starting to feel like I'm walking in a nightmare. It's when I accelerate toward the exit that I see the door marked 'Audio Sensory Awareness EPA'.

No-one responds to my knock. From where I'm standing the sound doesn't even penetrate. I can't hear anyone moving behind it, although, it could be a room within a room, or everyone could be wearing headphones, or the walls could be soundproof to prevent distractions, or none of that. The possibilities were endless really, like perhaps it's uninhabited and this is where they keep the brooms.

It feels too early to concede to a fruitless mission at such an inconvenient hour. The underpasses have wiped me out and it's wet, so the roads require twenty percent extra effort that I'd not yet regenerated. I'd rather wait for some fruit or get bored enough that agitation ensues which would be fuel enough to carry me home, so I sit in the alcove a few doors down, slide down the wall, studying my shoes wondering where all the mud came from.

It's hard to tell if I fell asleep or not, but there's really no time to think about it. All I have time to register are a pair of velcro sandals and a pair of Hightops breezing by the alcove, gone in an instant.

Two men.

"Avoid speaking as long as you can. Try sitting in it for a while before you go to sleep. You live nearby, right?"

Hightops is doing the talking. Sandals doesn't answer. They're through a door before I can hear what happens next.

It probably would've been smarter to follow the facilitator (Hightops), since he'd be the one to approach for an appointment, but when they disperse east and northwest in the quad, I can't take my eyes off Sandals. He's floating along the path as if it's moving him. The quad is lit up from the rain which adds to the effect. He's effortlessly gliding through this optical illusion, this trick of light.

Of course I follow him. I have to. After a few blocks I realise what it is about his gait that makes him seem so light and lithe—he's leading with his chest like a string is attached to his heart pulling him forward.

Occasionally he'll graze his fingers along a hedge and often he'll tip his head back so he's looking to the sky. Sandals exhibits zero traces of handlebar shoulders which makes me wonder if perhaps I'd witnessed a drug deal and not the aftermath of an after-hour research study.

When we turn onto Stranton, he walks down a path leading to a beautiful apartment complex lit up gold from the inside. The front door requires no key and through the windows I see him walking up the stairs like he'd just returned from some other galaxy.

MECH INSTITUTE

The entrance to the Mech Institute is almost better than the gallery itself, and the slower one walks, the better the effect. Being mid-morning it's much too populated for my liking, but with eyes to the ceiling, which is adorned with lights and jaggered mirrors and complimentary shadows, one can drown out the majority. It's like a version of Amal has been here; one who's into discos and sharp edges and public recognition. The hues abstract the scene so white shirts and blouses light up green and complexions are homogenized which offers a very rare and hard to come by sense of potentiality if one lingers and concentrates long enough. For the most part though, everyone's moving quickly in an effort to get to where they're going, and in their haste, I swear, I'm invisible.

By my ankles is this little stick man about five inches tall running with a briefcase, projected from some unknown place. He's running and running but no-one else seems to notice him not getting very far at all. He's only visible during the daylight hours I've noticed—a joke someone on my wavelength is playing.

If all the people walking were thoughts and all the lights were ideas, and the little man running is a dream trying to get somewhere, it'd be an exact representation of an artists psyche about to break out into a whole establishment of finished products.

After a brief flick through of the booklet the elderly man in overalls passes to everyone as they enter, I conclude either zero of the art pieces were by Harris Parchment, if he chose to use his real name, or two art pieces in particular, if he did not. It could've been any of them if that were the case, but these two stood out against the rest.

First is this exhibition; three and a half rooms devoted to work by a James Tushen—or so the brochure says. The exhibition is called Retrace which is one reason I think James is Harris. The other reason is because in the booklet there's one of his photos and it's a photo of a broken watch face.

At the entrance of the exhibition, this friendly looking mum-type wearing a name badge imprinted WENDY stops me and tells me she's about to conduct a tour. Since I have no prior commitments I tell Wendy I'll take part and she is delighted. She recruits five women other women, aged thirty plus. Only two of these women seem to know each other—a mum and daughter combo. No one else walks by for about two minutes so Wendy decides to commence the tour.

This fellow, James Tushen, does mostly photographs in black and white. Three of the four black walls host frames, seven pieces all up. The other wall is empty and unlit with a passageway to beyond.

One of the first pictures is a dead crow in the middle of the road. Wendy tells us it was taken in front of James' childhood home. She speaks a lot of conjecture about what things could mean and raises many questions about the dead crow and how represenative it is of the dark times that James experienced in his home.

"What's really interesting about this collection is Tushen's use of nature in all his photographs, particularly deadened plants and animals. It raises questions about his concentration on death as he's venturing into his past."

I'm looking at this dead bird feeling like someone who handled the art of parlay with a grace like no other would've found something else to photograph when he arrived at his childhood home after so many years.

"Have you met this James fellow?" I ask Wendy. Everyone looks at me like I've sworn in church.

"Yes?"

"I ask because I'm wondering if he feels any better now, having retraced his steps?"

The groups attention defers to my outfit so I look over Wendy's shoulder at a picture of a shard of glass on a tiled floor.

"I guess what he's doing is revisiting these places so he can make peace with these moments, so more of the good memories can come through."

"Isn't that just perpetuating the negative?"

Wendy turns her attention to the shard of glass picture.

"I speak with a lot of artists in my job and most often they have this subject they wish to explore, like a call to move something beyond a construct in their head, so they do what they can to heed the call, and whatever comes of it, is."

It's a nice sentiment Wendy's offering, but I came in search of answers not more questions, so I decide I'll give her one more room before I re-evaluate my commitment to the tour. She looks every member of our ad-hoc group in the eye to make sure they're still with her.

"Shall we continue?"

The next room is larger. It makes the first room look like the foyer. It's still dark, but the ceilings are much higher and there's a foot-thick partition dividing the room just off centre.

More nostalgic photographs hang solemn on the walls; the interior of an old car, a saturated baseball field, a torn piece of wallpaper and the smashed-face watch stuck on eleven thirty.

When we arrive on the east side to face the partition, we're faced with this projection of a looping scene flashing between a rainforest downpour and an atomic bomb spreading over dirt. At the bottom of the screen is a blown up shadow of the top of Wendy's head. The mother of the other woman doesn't care for it at all, she's busy playing with her bracelets, looking sad, if not shameful. This is the point where I float to the back of the pack and exit where we started.

The second is this piece which I suspect could be Harris is by Jose Raphelo. Even though it's spelled with a J, Jose has an H sound which is closer to Harris than James, but it's not so much the name as it is the picture itself. It's about as big as Selby's map drawings in it's size, that being about the width of two cards car and two Zac's high, but it's of this guy's face, made up of dots. Clusters of dots to make the lip section and the eyebrow section and his hair and his nose.

The gallery people have marked a line which is supposedly the perfect distance to view the picture from, and next to the line is a table with a sketchbook on it, containing various similar pictures by Jose. His style is to add a heap of noise to the photos so they're all black and white dot people.

In the front section of the notebook Jose writes a note about this piece. He says the work stems from a project where he stood on this one street corner for three months and took photos of random people as they went about their day. The guy on the wall is 15th June 2012, Fairmont, 12:04pm.

I don't care much what the official gallery people think about the best way to view Jose's work; I walk right up to the picture so I'm a foot away and look up at all these dots.

THE ESTHER

The bouncer doesn't believe my name to be Amina, and I guess I can't blame him. I'm about to rebut one last time when Jimmy appears and distracts him with a secret handshake. Apparently he's got some sway, and the bouncer makes an exception.

The place stinks of sweat, fake fog, and so much cologne I get an instant headache. Glazed eyes and big smiles. No smiles and closed eyes. So much drunk it's absorbent from proximity alone. Swaying bodies press together while lights flash messages soothing wasted thought patterns and faults of the day. It's too hectic to think and so foreign I could be anyone. So far I've been Amina, and the possibilities were endless.

Tanzania's in the middle of the dance-floor so far gone his eyes aren't open. His hair puts on a light show of green and blue and everyone blurs around him. I'm half-way over to him when some blonde guy gets in my face and starts yelling greetings at me. I yell back at him what could be German or Dutch, then point over toward the bar where this buff guy in a very tight shirt thinks I'm pointing at him. Blonde guy looks confused, then wary, then distances himself per strobe flash. Jimmy soon replaces him. He has a drink in his hand, something and coke or just coke, and his sideburns are tracking more of his jawline than the last time I saw him. I bow down to bridge the distance and ask him if he knew where I could find Harris Parchment. He either said, *'he's right over there,'* or *'what's wrong with your hair'* and then moves me out of the way and heads toward the stage, leaving me standing there, looking around for someone who I don't know what he looks like, too tired to be anyone, let alone myself. Space fills up around me, so I dance one song with vigour which is all it takes to feel satisfied with the experience. No-one knew how drunk I wasn't.

AMYGDALA

I've become something of a prisoner in an unlocked house. No kids in the schoolyard and yesterday's word remains untouched in the fence. Jojo isn't around to amuse me either; just some less enthused dogs with less enthused owners and Thermos Man in his usual spot. The park is plastered with young leaves from days and nights of pelting rain.

Gustave's asleep in a pool of light on the top step. Occasionally his tag scrapes against the wood. Beside me, my pedestal fan rotates left to right, replicating my mood precisely.

It's in my transition from Wall Ball to Rubber Band Game that I notice Allan looking through my bedroom window. He doesn't say hello or excuse himself when I open the front door to let him in, instead he beelines it by me, straight down the hall, with his toolbox in tow. Evidently, he knew exactly the location of the laundry cupboard from the time he came to reinforce the fly screen on the back door and ended up just taking it off completely and not replacing it at all.

By the time I reach the kitchen, Allan's reaching up to inspect the problem exposing a gaunt hip and a strip of white cotton underwear.

"No problem. Easy fix."

"Do you want a glass of water or something?"

"No time."

He kneels next to his toolbox and opens out its multi-leveled compartments. I figure he'd hate it if I watched him work, and I'm hoping for a swift repair, so I retreat to the couch and flip open one of Zac's books called Einstein's Dreams, presumably about Einstein's dreams. On my fourth attempt trying to cohere the first sentence, Allan speaks again.

"Day off today?"

"Yeah."

"No work?"

"No."

"No school?"

"No."

Allan's opening and closing the laundry door in a vigorous manner. On the fifth repeat, the roller he's there to reinforce bounces once on the kitchen floor, twice on the living room floor, then rolls down the floorboards according to the slant until it reaches its final destination well under Zac's desk.

I roll off the couch and reach through lint and bottle caps and cables to retrieve the roller for him. We meet at the kitchen doorway and I drop the roller in his weathered hand. It looks like his fingernails haven't been cut since the second time he ever visited the barber. They're curved, yellow, rough and corrugated.

"You're on unstable ground," he says, grey eyes pressing into mine.

"Pardon?"

He moves by me to the couch, then drops to the floor like he's just noticed an infrared target on his chest. His nose is inches from the floorboards. He holds out the roller and releases it. After a moment gaining momentum, it rolls under Zac's desk again.

"What's this a ten, fifteen percent tilt?"

"I don't think it's that bad."

He looks over his shoulder.

"Oh, but it is."

"Are you able to fix it?" I ask. "The laundry door I mean?"

Swiftly, he's up on his feet. He retrieves the roller and dusts off his shorts.

"Yes absolutely."

I sit down on the couch again and he goes to the kitchen.

"You're home all alone?" he asks.

"Today I am."

Holding Einstein above my head isn't helping my handlebar shoulders, so I put the book on my stomach, and watch it rise but not really fall. Soon enough, Allan appears.

"Got any cotton wool?" he asks.

Far be it from me to question his methods, I head to the bathroom, extract few white clouds of cotton from the bathroom cabinet and present him the fluff. He grabs them and turns his attention back to the laundry door situation. I figure he'll probably get the job done quicker without me in his line of sight, so I head for the balcony.

Many doors down some unseen neighbours are in the middle of what sounds like an entertaining luncheon. Knives and forks scrape on plates, someone cracks a can of something fizzy. Nearer that, Selby's washing blows in the breeze, more above the line than below it. No action in The Dope Haus. Gustave's climbing up the fire escape to greet me.

"Beautiful day, isn't it?" Allan calls.

"Allan," I reply. "What would you do if you could gain unofficial access to a location that housed private information that could potentially ease a good percentage of your woes?"

Gustave turns and descends the fire escape and Allan doesn't respond. It might've been because halfway through my question Allan drops what sounds like a whole bucket of screws on the floor. At the very same time, a pair of Selby's undies fly off the line and stick to a vine about a third of the way down The Dope Haus's fence.

By the time I get down there it's Eyebrows and Clive and no oven in sight. They don't notice I've seen them. They're on the porch. Eyebrows is in trackpants and a hoodie. Clive is in basketball shorts and no shirt.

"Centre most core of your brain," Eyebrows says. "The amygdala. Shape of an almond. You can make magic from there."

"Which part do you destroy a relationship from?"

"Are we still on that?"

"Seems so."

"It's been a long ride for you. Aren't you tired?"

So tired Clive needs some time to think about it.

"I'm stuck," he says finally.

"You've gotta see the bigger picture man. You've been repeating the same story for months now. You need a new perspective."

"It's all I think about."

"I know, it's all we hear about. I have this image of ticker-tape going around in your head. It's got these three—no, four—subjects on repeat: that girl, food, basketball and your mum."

"That's not... incorrect. How is Marguerite though? She looked good the last time I saw her."

"Ah, don't do that to me man. I'm only trying to help. Besides, have you ever tried taking your own advice? It's impossible."

In my absence, Allan vacated the premises. At first I thought he left me a note with the answer to my question, but on closer inspection it appears Zac has simply circled the already bold and capitalised due date on the latest electric bill. Halfway down the page in the white space he scrawled:

LA VIGNETTE ?PM. PMP.

Careful not to ruin his penmanship, I rip a section from the bill the size of a business card and write 'amygdala' on it, then move the beluga from the bottom left section of the fridge to central eye level, positioning the bill underneath it and the sunflower magnet on top.

On my way to the front door, Allan's Phillips-head screwdriver stabs me in the foot leaving a purple dent in my sole. Despite my distaste for him in the moment, I go to store his tool for safe keeping, only to find myself victim again when the right laundry door falls in, scarring the varnish on the other one even deeper. Moments later, an apparatus made of cotton wool tied with electrical tape with a pin sticking out of it falls on the lino and bounces once between my feet.

CENTRIFUGAL

Overhead is a clear summers night. No clouds in the sky, stars free to gaze upon. An inkling of urine taints the air as we wait for Alexis at the stage exit. Aaron's kicking stones. Dynamite's looking down the alleyway to the section of sidewalk where congregations of theatre goers are either relating, opinioning or looking for an escape.

"That's what I said—we'll see the play, then get a falafel," Aaron says.

"Now you're straight up lying. You mentioned nothing of a play."

"What's up with intermissions anyway?" Aaron queries. "It's like inviting people to leave."

The stage-exit opens and a pepper haired guy in black jeans appears. He seems surprised to see us waiting there, pausing to scope us out. After he deems us non-threatening he lights his smoke while his right boot keeps the door ajar.

"Why do you still think smoking is cool?" Aaron asks Dynamite, causing him to brew hot instantly. Dynamite's considering a powerful response when the door swings open surprising Pepperhead and Alexis emerges, walking towards us looking like he's either taken a horse tranquilizer or hasn't slept in days. His eyes are small and angry and his jaw is locked in place. He looks a lot like a simian.

"It's not going well, is it?" His voice is small and contained.

"Do you want the truth?" Dynamite asks.

"No, better not."

"Don't worry about your acting man," Aaron says, smile almost bigger than his face. "Look at your tights, that's what everyone is looking at."

Aaron pretends to pierce Alexis' gut with an imaginary sword. "You really showed that Cornelius guy."

Alexis doesn't respond to the stabbing, he's not quite in his body. He does clench his fists by his side though, then pushes his fingertips into his closed eyes.

"Rehearsal does absolutely nothing to prepare you for the real thing. It's like everyone is watching me, waiting for me to fuck-up."

"They're not interested in you," Dynamite says, smoke catching on the breeze. "They're interested in themselves. You're just involved in that for a minute. Forget them, their memory is flawed anyway."

It's indeterminable whether the advice makes its way to Alexis. He offers me an apologetic smile for his bad mood, so I smile back silentl telling him I understand and can relate completely.

"We're having celebratory drinks at our place after," he tells me. "They might be condolence drinks—we'll see how act two goes. Feel free to bring some female friends along—for Aaron."

Aaron's nodding, looking pretty happy to've been acknowledged. The three of us look at Dynamite who hasn't noticed we're all watching him watching the happenings down the alleyway. Eventually he tunes in and looks at each of us, smoke poised by his lips for another puff.

"What?"

"He's not here," Alexis tells him. "He never comes to the shows, but don't worry, he'll be at the house later, so you'll get your chance."

"I'm not going to say anything," Dynamite replies. "Well, maybe I'll say *one* thing."

"What's that?" Alexis asks.

"I just want to know if he's aware of it."

"Aware of what?"

"That he's omitted all the wrong scenes."

Alexis shakes his head tiny shakes.

"Do you realise how ridiculous you sound?"

"Do you?"

"How long do you guys think it would take to make a falafel?" Aaron asks. "More than ten minutes?"

Two bells break the tension rendering all their questions void. At the door, Pepperhead gives Alexis a two-fingered wave in to which Alexis responds with a deep breath out, then he presses down on Aaron's shoulder, nods to Dynamite and then to me, and heads back toward stage exit, tights glimmering as he goes.

Aaron leads the way down the alley but progress stops at the footpath where the masses bottleneck, waiting to get inside. In his efforts to stub out his smoke, Dynamite inadvertently cuts off a well-to-do grey haired woman unimpressed by his antics. He's not shy to mirror the same stale sentiment back to her.

Through the sea of people, a mess of familiar curls cuts through the crowd heading straight for me. Soon enough, the rest of Tanzania emerges and I'm telling him I'm good only about sixty percent sure he even asked how I was.

"I saw you and I thought— *hey, I know her.*"

"Spelling bee. Indolence. It's all coming back to me now."

"That's right. That's me. The spelling bee."

"I taught that word to some school kids."

"You did?"

"Well, I think so. I'm not sure if they got the message or not."

"What are you doing here?"

"Oh, my roommate is Regulus in this play."

"Selby is your roommate?"

"Yeah."

"No shit!"

"No, none."

Most of the patrons have been swallowed by the theatre with a few strays lingering by the doors immersed in their own self-made entertainment. A boy-sized man dressed in a fedora, suspenders and colourful socks is holding the door ajar, silently asking me if he should keep standing there. Tanzania's sitting on the top step now, either expecting me to follow or ambivalent about whether our reunion is over. I signal a *no* to Fedora and he dips his hat and goes inside.

"I'm about to smoke a joint if you'd like to join me?"

On that note, Tanzania withdraws a joint from his matted curls over his right ear. It's about as thick as my pinky finger.

"I can't," I tell him. "Practicing abstinence for a medical experiment I'm involved in."

"Cool, what's the experiment?"

"Perception in relation to motion."

"Sounds interesting."

"It's alright. It's the kind where one thing is happening, but it feels like something else is really going on."

"There's a good one at Hudson with a black dot."

"With Leonardo?"

"Yeah, cool guy, hey?"

I withhold my comment as he lights the joint by his knees because of the breeze. His hair's crowned gold on top from the light bulbs spelling out *La Vignette* overhead. He takes in a drag, then exhales. The smoke catches on the westerly.

"I saw you the other day—at The Esther."

"You did? And you didn't say hello?"

"I wasn't there long, and you were lost in the rhythym, I didn't want to disturb."

"You saw me dancing?"

"I did."

He laughs.

"I like that place. It reminds me of home, the music they play."

Neither of us says anything in the time it takes a cyclist to ride in and out of my periphery.

"So, you're a teacher?" he asks.

"No. What makes you say that?"

"You said you taught some kids the word indolence."

"Oh, right. No. I just put scraps of paper in schoolyard fences with interesting words on them for kids to read and learn."

"Is that right? Why do you do that?"

"At first it was an effort to encourage them to subvert the system, but that seems misguided now."

He coughs out a laugh. "What bought you to that conclusion?"

"I was watching this woman eating a sandwich one day and I realised how stressed my teachers must've been. Most of them weren't very happy at all looking back."

His eyebrows tells me he's absorbed the information, and can relate,but this time he withholds his comment and responds by taking another drag.

"Are you finding the play that bad?" I ask him.

He exhales and smiles, flicking ash and twisting the joint between his fingertips.

"I'm sure it's really good if you've lived every variable of the playwright's life."

"What do you think the paper mache parasols are all about?"

He considers my question while taking another drag.

"There's no symbolic meaning. I just liked the way the words looked on the page."

The sentiment lands as the smoke dissolves and his left brow lifts with amusement at my expression. He laughs out some residue.

"Don't worry," He rubs my right shoulder. "It's all good."

"I'm so sorry. It's really good, it is."

"Honestly, don't worry about it."

"I just get wound up sitting shoulder to shoulder with strangers, then I saw you, and well, it's such a nice night and we were just talking about why intermissions exist at all and—"

"I agree, it is a beautiful night."

He seems sincere, smiling as he watches the activity unfold on the street below. Focusing on the streetlights is a nice distraction from the heat in my face, and chlorine residue from the afternoon sends beams of streetlight over the scene. One points directly to a puppeteer by the doors of the metro who's having his own intermission, and some yoghurt.

"It's all pretty sweet, isn't it?" He juts his chin toward the bustle. "You kinda think they've read the script, but they haven't. Up close you can see how they might take a wide berth on a perceived lower socio-economic individual, but that's the trouble with attention to detail, you end up seeing each brushstroke and not the whole painting."

I feel like he's refering to the lightness to the evening only a weekend could provide. There's a certain dance to it; this perfectly timed flow which has space for everyone to get to where they're going with no notable collisions. Individual conversations fuse into a hum, accented with horns, bus brakes and the occasional name call. Tanzania ashes the joint, then checks to see if I'm sure I don't want any.

"I really did enjoy the first half of your play." I tell him. "I like that line that Cornelius character said—about the future, and how it's not coming all at once."

"You did, huh?"

"I do the same thing."

"What's that?"

"Just stand there feeling so overwhelmed by it all that I do nothing at all."

He looks at me, his eyes glistening, glassy and shrunken considerably since we sat down. He's smiling just the same.

"Well, there's a lot to choose from and that can paralyse a person. Usually it does, but our needs are pretty simple when you get down to it, and I think that's what's hardest to swallow."

"Are you talking about Maslow?"

"I don't know Maslow, I just mean we overcomplicate everything by being so absorbent, so susceptable to influence, but there comes a point where you know what you need to do and it's a decision you need to make for yourself. No-one else is gonna give you the answers you want."

It's exactly the opposite of what I want to hear. The bad news carries on the westerly to annoy those at the lookout on top of the mountain.

"It makes we wanna call out—*don't worry everyone, you're getting exactly what you've asked for. Everything you want—it's coming. Just chill.*"

"Why don't you?"

"Well, they're the crazy ones, aren't they?" He straightens up like he's about to do it. "Will you do it with me?"

"No. No way."

"Why not? C'mon—if you do something rebellious by yourself, you're crazy. If you do something rebellious with someone else, you're rebels."

"Is that how it goes?"

"Something like that."

Tanzania deflates, forgoing the idea, and positions the joint by his lips, then he changes his mind and blunts it by his right foot and points the stump in the direction of the bus parked on the other side of the street.

"Speaking of rebels, have you gone to see Amina?"

"She's in the bus?"

"No silly, in the hotel."

"Oh, right. That's the Majesty. Didn't even compute."

"Scored myself some complimentary socks."

He notices me taking stock of his bare feet, so he taps on the right pocket of his cargo shorts which bulges out about the width of some rolled-up socks. It sparks my wondering of what all his other pockets contain, but my reverie is cut short by the snap of metal behind me. I turn to find Dynamite at the main entrance, bending down to inspect the lower hinges of one of the doors. He tries to close it but it makes an uncomfortable clicking sound which has him avoiding any follow-up efforts. He's checking for witnesses and that's when he notices us. With options limited, he heads in our direction, positioning a smoke in his mouth on his way. He sits on Tanzania's right side.

"Can't fucking breathe in there. The clown *next to me* is breathing *directly* on my hand like he's *aiming for it* and why are the chairs so *fucking close together*?"

He notices the scent on the breeze and studies the surroundings until he locates the half-done bat between Tanzania's fingers. His eyes light up like Aaron's are usually.

"Is that a spliff?"

An exchange is made and Dynamite re-ignites the joint, taking a deep draw.

"Thanks man. That's exactly what I needed. Nice parasol analogy—very clever."

Tanzania nudges me with his elbow and nods his head in agreeance, catering to the pair of us. Dynamite returns the joint and Tanzania takes another drag.

"Fuck! Now I feel like a dick for leaving."

"Nah, it's all good brother. It's only got about two minutes left."

Dynamite looks perturbed.

"Wasn't it just intermission? Or is this really strong weed?"

Tanzania smiles, offering Dynamite another hoot.

"Both. It's a surprise. People are going to be happy they've got more of the night to enjoy what they're about to hear."

"What are they about to hear?"

"I'd tell you, but then no-one would buy tickets tomorrow."

"*Fuck!*"

Dynamite's agitated gesture causes him to lose his smoke. It rolls down two steps before getting lodged in a crack. He gets up to retrieve it displaying a puff of plain white boxers.

"No worries man, it's on for the next three weeks. You're on the door whenever you want. You too miss."

Tanzania scans the entrance behind him. No-one is around. The door's still wide open and I'm tempted to go back inside. The thought of being ambushed by a stampede of theatre-goers wasps away the desire as quick as it arrives.

"I'm actually expecting some harsh backlash about it, so it's high time I head out of here. That puppermaster down there usually has some Triptochen stuffed up the arses of those birds. You're both welcome to join me if you want?"

Dynamite's quick to his feet, a little unsteady.

"I'll come for the encounter, but I can't stay for the drugs."

Tanzania nods.

"And you miss?"

I shake my head.

"I think I'll go see Amina. I'm supposed to recruit some girls."

"Who's Amina?" Dynamite asks.

"An Arabian princess who lives in the Majesty Hotel," Tanzania tells him.

"Now let's go. The birds are on the move."

OASIS

Amina's behind the reception desk serving a couple dressed in khakis. She's alert to my presence instantly, and with a head-tilt she indicates I should sit on the black couches in the middle of the lobby until she's finished serving the khaki couple.

By her side is a male collegue, about twenty-years. He's bright red and intently focused on the screen in front of him while this guy in a shiny blue suit looks around the lobby looking pretty vexed. He steps up to the counter.

"I don't get how hard it is to find a reservation? I would think a confirmation number usually implies the reservation is confirmed, wouldn't you?"

The khaki couple are leaning away from this guy like he's emitting a foul odour, and I must've been offering even worse feedback, because he shoots me a look that says, *what, bitch?* so I defer my attention to the function room double doors so I can watch the scene unfold in reverse.

Young Concierge slips through the γlno ‡‡ɒtɀ doors, either to consult a higher managerial power or take a solitary moment of recovery. Amina's giving Blue Suit the deathstare as he paces the lobby venting his frustrations to someone on the phone. The Khaki's ask her a question and her face smooths out and she mouths, *sorry?*

Meanwhile a young couple exit the elevators, taking a wide berth on Blue Suit, venturing nearer the other side of the hall by the ornate dresser decorated with one of those ancient dial-up phones that'd take me about seventeen minutes to dial all the necessary prefixes to reach my parents.

The Khaki couple head toward the revolving door and Amina makes her way across the lobby. It's not until she's up-close that I notice she's certainly looking the part; red lipstick, hair smoothed down more than I thought would be possible.

"You look real fancy," I tell her.

"Oh please, they basically force me to make an effort."

"They force you?"

"On my first shift my boss is like, *Amina, we like you, but we have to talk about your hair.*" She clasps her hands together. "So, what's happening?"

"I was across the street watching your friend's play."

"Which friend?"

"Tanzania."

"I have no idea who that is."

"You know, spelling bee guy."

"Oh, you mean Harris? From *Trinidad.*"

"You're kidding?"

"Yeah, Trinidad and Tobago."

"Harris? As in Harris Parchment?"

Amina searches my face for signs of injury. "Are you ok?"

"I think I've been hit by a dart."

"You're not making any sense."

I look around the lobby for answers and find Blue Suit pacing near the luggage trolley. It looks like whomever he's talking to isn't impressing him much either. Amina takes my hand and leads me to the couches, then smoothes out her skirt and sits on the edge. I slump next to her looking up to the chandelier glinting every colour. The jewels are held together by cobwebs.

"Now, who is Tanzania and what's this about a play?"

"Tanzania is Harris—who wrote a play."

She looks back at the reception desk where her young colleague is now shadowed by an older man dressed the same as him but about four sizes larger. He looks to be taking command of the situation. tempering Blue Suit with subdued tone. The kid's complexion has reduced to a pale pink.

"Now that you say that, he did mention something about a production. Sometimes I can't hear him very well. What was it like?"

"Well, I didn't see the whole thing but from what I understand he's quite the innovator. It's probably really good if you've lived every variable of his life."

"Are you on something?"

"What? No, why? Does it seem like I am?"

"You seem on edge."

"I can't believe... doesn't matter."

I rearrange upright so she doesn't attract too much attention for hosting a drifter, and at the same time, a middle-aged couple enters through the revolving doors, stumbling while holding each other up, unquestionably on their way to have drunken sex.

I shake my head to clear a new trajectory for our conversation while Blue Suit makes his way to the elevator with a small suitcase reluctantly following him. When he looks in our direction the suitcase flips up onto one wheel and hits him in the Achilles. Amina waits until he's by the lifts before she celebrates the moment.

"I'm told some cast drinks are due to go down on the other side of town by Uscray soon, can you come?"

"I'll be here 'til five," She tells me, then suddenly looks surprised. "But hey, if you've got a minute you should head up to the tenth floor."

"Why?"

"One minute, I'll come with you. Can you wait a minute?"

"Can I wait a minute near a phone that'll let me make a long-distance call?"

"Right this way ma'am."

She's on her feet, arms outstretched so she can pull me up too. We're heading toward the elevators when a man in a beige suit approaches tentatively. The suit's made of hemp or some other natural fibre which has him looking like he repairs watches for a living in the backstreets of Panama. His eyes shift over the black and white tiles between our feet pairs.

"Uh, excuse me miss?"

"Yes, Mr Lebosh?" Amina uses her service voice as she bows slightly in an effort to meet his height.

"Sorry to bother you. I wonder if you can help me and my—uh—fiancé. We locked ourselves out of my—uh—our room."

"I can absolutely help you with that, Mr Lebosh." She turns to me and lowers her tone. "Tenth floor, and take a left passed the ice machine. Press 0-3-1 to dial out."

⬦

Fifteen rings later and it crackles, then static and then... silence.

"Dad?"

"I can't really talk right now Lou. My phone's dying and I'm only half sure I know where I'm going."

Great.

"I've been walking in circles for almost an hour and I've got a flashing bar. Can you hear it beeping?"

"Are you sure it's not a truck reversing with an elephant in it?"

"No, it's my phone. Your mum says hi. We're happ— So— Yo— You're jo—"

Beeeeeeeeep.

"Hello?"

The silence tapers off and one ding later, the lift doors open and I'm pleased to find it's Amina. She points down the hall.

"This way."

I follow her down the corridor and into a different alcove. She pushes down on the handle but the door doesn't open. From her back pocket she retrieves a key card which grants her the green light. The door opens and the warmth of the night ten stories up engulfs me.

The first thing I notice is the smell of chlorine, then sandstone pavers lead to a pool of turquoise, completely calm and glowing bright, surrounded by palms tinted blue from underneath. Inch thick glass borders the east and west walls, and the north wall is sandstone bricks with uplighting. In the distance, neighbourhoods glitter shades of yellow and pearl white while a helicopter chops overhead.

It's like she's transported me to a mirage; the kind kept secret amongst locals and even they only visit on cosmic occasions to preserve the magic.

"Pretty cool huh?"

Amina's entering the garden bed on the east side leaning behind an urn as tall as her and three times as wide. A murmur starts, and then a stream of water spits, then flows from the decorative panel on the north wall into the pool. It adds a serene trickling to the scene which does something to soften the area where I imagined my amygdala to be.

"So you do your swimming here?" I ask her. "Off-peak?"

She adjusts a pre-folded towel to double thickness and sits on the edge of a deck chair, then kicks her shoes off, flexing her toes, pressing them into the pavers.

"Management and I have an arrangement." she tells me. "It's one of the perks

THE TROUBLE WITH NOUNS

of the job and a good reason why I still work here."

"I hope these extra guest services don't get you fired."

"Nah, my boss loves me."

On the pool floor, little black square tiles create a perfect circle of the Majesty logo, lit up by eight lights running the length of each side, focused centrally. The water's warm on my fingertips, beckoning entry. The ripples slowly make their way over to her side of the pool.

"I hope that Colin kid isn't too distressed."

"Who's Colin?"

"Your colleague down there getting served by that jerk."

"Ah, Chris," she laughs out her nose. "Do you make up people's names to suit yourself?"

"I saw a 'C' and five or so blurry letters."

"If I know Steve—aka management—Chris's probably on his third finger of scotch right now and has a real fun night ahead of him involving light duties and some sort of wastebasket oriented competition."

Beyond the glass wall on the north-west side, the mountain is shadowed like a purging wave. A few tiny people adorn the balustrade on the lookout, and a few blocks over, some slightly larger people are drinking on a rooftop. They don't see me wave.

"I don't know how you deal with it."

"With their games? I referee sometimes. It's light fun."

"No, people like that."

"Ah." Amina pushes herself off the deckchair and walks on her toes to the edge of the pool. The glow of turquoise darkens her lips to almost black which makes her look much older than when she was downlit by the chandelier. Not older like she's aged, just... more refined. She tip-toes the edge toward the north end. I flick of my shoes and do the same on the opposite side, mirroring her.

"It used to bug me, but now I see the other side of it. Most people are real sweet and friendly but yeah, there's the occasional few. That guy down there, losing his cool like that, I find it so interesting to watch."

"I couldn't deal with it. It'd be too hard for me to bite my tongue."

"I find when you're composed, they don't know what to do. They're so used to people biting back, so I listen to them and watch them jolt when I respond with understanding. The shock of it pacifies them... usually. "

She's looking passed the surface into the depths of the pool, to some other place.

"But hey, who am I to judge. They've walked their path, I've walked mine. And really, I have no idea what's going on behind the scenes." She looks across the pool at me. "Well, sometimes I do. Like Mr Lebosh and his—" she quotes "*fiancé*."

When we reach the north end she does a one-eighty, heading back where she came from. I do the same. Turquoise on my left, pavers on my right.

"You really left when things got interesting Lou. I think I've learnt more these last four weeks than the last three years put together."

"Why do you think that is?"

"Could be any number of things: great profs, good topics, dots joining. Maybe it's not that I'm learning more, more like... it all feels like it's settling in."

She looks at me like she's about to ask something, but no words cross the pool. She starts walking the edge again.

"What is it?" I ask.

"What?"

"It looked like you were going to say something."

"I was."

"Just ask."

"Do you know what I was going to ask?"

"I have an idea."

"Well?"

A flow of information travels over the pool's surface and her hypothesis is confirmed in a heartbeat. On receipt, she looks to the pavers and nods subtly to herself—an act I appreciate and admire. I retreat inward a paver because my position on the edge is no longer safe.

"You can't let that take you over Lou. None of us knew. That'd be like me blaming myself for where Amal is. I was absolutely a contender and it makes me sick to think about it, but who's it gonna help? All it'll do is suck you in and render you useless."

"What do you mean? Where's Amal?"

"Back home."

"What? Why?"

She shakes her head.

"It's like what I was saying before about watching people here—it's all over their face, in the way they walk, how they react. I should've seen it, but sometimes you're too close, you know? You were with Owen. I was too. But blaming yourself isn't going to bring him back and holding it in is just going to manifest you into a distorted shape."

The developments have left me lightheaded, and suddenly I feel a wave of vertigo so I sit on the pavers and roll out onto my stomach so my head is over the water, inches from my face. Amina's stopped too. She's standing on the edge of the pool with her toes hanging over, up lit and polished. I have no idea what I look like to her, lying on my stomach looking up at her across the pool like I am.

"Like RSI," I tell her.

"What's RSI?"

"Repetitive stress injury."

"Oh right. Yes exactly. That's exactly what it is. Mental RSI. Blame, shame and guilt."

Water glistens between us and she meets my eye.

"You're self-sabotaging," she tells me.

"I know. I can't help but feel it though."

"How many levels deep do you feel it?"

"Haven't counted."

She smiles, steps back on her left foot and launches into the pool, swallowed by a delicate splash. All that remains is the sound of water lapping the walls and the fountain's stream meeing the surface. In her absense I locate zero traces of any other level other than the all-encompassing one.

When she resurfaces, her hair reflects the sky's black and drops fall from her face. A few strokes later we're face to face and she's treading water, holding onto the edge.

"Are you just gonna look at it, or are you coming in?"

FORTUITY

The opportunity presented before me really was a now-or-never kind of scenario. My hope is the energy from the show carries over to levels of drunk and jovality that'd be easy enough to stealth my way through.

The door is ajar when I arrive, so I enter on the pretence that such behaviours are generally acceptable when it comes to social gatherings. I'm walking the hall expecting to hear a medley of voices lifting and lingering but the place is dead silent. When I get to the living space it's only Dynamite at the kitchen table reading a novel with a box of cereal on his lap. He looks me up and down, doesn't say a thing.

"Oh, uh... isn't there supposed to be some sort of gathering? Alexis said—"

"Change of plans. They went to some bar on Lincoln."

"Right."

The home phone rings obnoxious and shrill. He puts the cereal box on the table and gets up to answer it.

"Hey, do you mind if I use your bathroom before I go?"

"Yeah, I don't care." He picks up the phone. "What?"

On the way to the bathroom I find myself at the helm of a current too powerful to avoid. It encourages me to take a hard right directly into Alexis' room. I slide through the opening and switch on the light.

The first thing I see is a tiger jumping through a velour blanket on the east wall, then an amass of what looks like four duvets thrown over a piano. Clothes decorate most surfaces and next to my right hip is a glass jar with a mix of keys and cards; both business and plastic. The M-13 card is right on top, then it's in my back pocket.

As I position the door in the exact position as it was before my interference, I hear him clear his throat behind me in a very deliberate and questioning manner. Dynamite's silence is the question.

"I'm borrowing a key to break into a university research facility."

His expression gives nothing away.

"I'll come with you."

COVERT

The climb up the incline doesn't shed any light on Dynamite's motives. Not a word crosses between us the whole journey to campus providing me with too much headspace to question the main flaws of the mission; those being, its entirety.

Fireflies of apprehension sit at the base of my ribs. With every streetlight certainty fades, and yet—we advance.

Dynamite looks pretty mad to be there. I can't figure out why he wanted to come. His right ear is pierced twice but holds no earrings.

"How was the puppet experience?"

"Bullshit."

"Why was it bullshit?"

He shakes his head. "It's not worth explaining."

"Why not?"

"You'd have to know what he's like, or what he was like."

"What he was like?"

Dynamite frowns at the footpath.

"Not like he was tonight, talking all nonchalant to that fuckin' puppet guy."

He's walking ahead of me now, fire in his steps. Somehow he knows where we're going and speed is probably in our best interest.

"Nonchalant how?"

"Fuckin'... spilling shit about how the play was channelled through him. Basically taking no responsibility for it at all."

"I didn't get that impression."

"What about how he abandons the cast, doesn't even watch it? He's seen the light and now he's an island."

"Maybe he's just self-conscious."

Dynamite scoffs at my suggestion and I slow down because we're at the double doors. Lights glow bright white from inside shedding too much light on the absurdity of the situation.

I definitely don't feel like an island. Maybe a rock thrown toward a body of water about to breach the surface.

Dynamite's standing by the bike rack ten feet away like some forcefield is preventing any forward motion. He checks the vacant quad behind him, the left side of his face shadowed, then the right.

The whole scene is dream-like; the absence of people. The space around us. Stillness in the air. Consequences pending.

"What are we doing here exactly?"

"We're searching for a hidden document that's going to set me free."

He nods and clears his throat. "Yeah, see, this whole scenario seemed much more enthralling in the safety of my own home. I think I might go."

"Okay. Do that."

When I open the door, Dynamite takes two steps closer, then does a U-turn so he's back in the same spot. He's torn.

"Look, if we get caught, start speaking German and I'll start crying, then we're just some sorry foreign kids who took too many wrong turns. We'll act drunk even. It might be a stretch, but I could probably muster up that kind of energy if the situation calls for it."

"Yes, because being drunk is a solid defense."

His chest increases ten percent like he's activated an internal shield.

"You're very debonair about this," he tells me.

"Debonair?"

He glares at my amusement. Mostly amused I could be amused.

"Are you coming or not?"

He scratches his head and doesn't answer, so I make his choice for him. I figure I would've already made it to Rachel's office by now without all this talk, so I enter the doors and feel them seal behind me.

To compensate for lost time, I take two steps per stride which seems like a good idea considering the circumstances, but exhaustion comes quick as a result. Breath heavy. Legs heavy. Every platform between flights marks another unsafe haven, and the fluorescent lights eradicate all traces of stealth mode I'd been using to fuel the mission so far.

Footsteps from above, behind—I can't tell.

"What floor?" Dynamite's question carries through the stairwell with ease, which fills me with un-ease.

"Six," I tell him. He passes me easily, executing the two step approach with much more finesse.

Stairs. Platform. Stairs. Platform. Stairs.

He waits at the entrance to the sixth floor transit zone so I can enter first. How considerate. The area's unlit, somewhat comforting, but only for a moment because the motion sensors activate the lights. We're quick through the east door, heading down the corridor while red sensors blink warnings above us. We pass trolleys pushed to walls topped with tubes and metallic instruments.

"What's your name again?" he asks between footsteps.

"Are you serious?" My whisper comes out a hiss.

"Yes, I'm serious."

"I'd prefer not to answer that in this environment."

In front of Rachel's door, the fireflies relocate to the place I imagine my spleen to be. They join wing to wing, locking my shoulders secure as concrete so my heartbeat has nowhere to go. I put the card against the white box but it doesn't beep. I try flipping the card—nothing.

Again—nothing. We look at each other, stunted.

"What now?" he asks.

"I guess we go."

Dynamite looks back down the empty hall grazing his thumb and forefinger along his jaw line which makes a sound like rough sandpaper. In this light, I notice how the furrow between his eyebrows is beginning to imprint as a permanent fixture. He notices me noticing, then leans in and tries the door handle. It clicks open.

"Simplicity is key," he says.

The PSOH folder is right there on the desk like Rachel knew I was coming and is trying to make it easy for me. The baby keeps quiet about the infiltration and the ghost version of me sits in the visitor's chair looking flushed, sweaty and insecure. I sit on her and open the folder.

Dynamite's looking up at the certificates on the wall as I flick through the questionnaires. His presence is reassuring in a sense.

If you do something rebellious by yourself, you're crazy. If you do something rebellious with someone else, you're rebels.

"This Rachel Alvarez certainly has a lot of posters of herself," he tells me.

I'm flipping through the forms trying, trying, trying to concentrate.

Fletcher.

Fletcher.

Owen Fletcher.

I'm up to K when he moves behind my right shoulder to see what I'm doing.

"What are those?"

"They're questionnaires for a research experiment."

"What kind of experiment?"

"A speech perception experiment."

He backs away a step. "Are you looking for an ex's new address? Because I don't know if I can stand here and allow that. I knew a guy—"

"No. It's not like that."

"What's it like then?"

It's not here.

As I re-flick through A - M, he walks around the desk and sits in Rachel's chair. Something about the way he puts his feet up on the corner makes me mad, but obviously I have no grounds to lecture him about respectful conduct. Instead, I spread the forms out across the desk hoping a different angle might help.

"Can you see a Fletcher?"

Dynamite looks around the room, likely for the reason he'd come this far. Whatever he settled on, he didn't consider it bad. He moves his feet to the floor and respositions himself over the spread for a better view.

"Is that the first name?" he asks.

"No. Owen. Owen Fletcher."

"What do you have to do for it?"

"Do for what?"

"The experiment."

"Oh. So far I've said some words into a mircophone. Hid, Head, Hid, Head."

"What's the point of that?"

"Something about how when you repeat the same thing again and again it eventually loses its meaning and doesn't even sound like words anymore."

He picks up a form and holds it between us so that it curves over his hands and covers the bottom half of his face. His eyelids glow red, like he's been rubbing them, or, because of the weed.

"If this guy isn't a victim of a tainted love affair, who is he?"

"I know him. Well, I used to know him."

Over the form he shoots me a look telling me the explaination is insufficient.

"We had class together, a few over the years and then one day he didn't come back."

"Like he dropped out or something?"

"You could say that."

He puts the form down and looks over the rest of them, selecting another one.

"There's no Fletcher." I tell him.

"There really isn't."

That's it. Verdict is in. I'm officially off the rails. The walls start closing in. I start compiling the forms with haste. "Okay, let's go. Bad, bad idea."

"Not now, I found a good one. It's Louise right? Louise Beckman?"

"I thought you didn't know my name."

"It's not so nice when the tables are turned, is it?"

"I think we're way passed that point now."

"Louise Beckman. 389 Delisle. Ticked no to drugs. Rates high for anxiety and claustrophobia. No to hallucinations." He looks at me over the form. "Well that's not entirely true, is it?"

He flips to the second page and reclines, looking smug as hell.

"How interesting... "

"What?"

"Says here, *ask about the girl in chains*."

"No idea. I didn't write it. Give it back. We should go."

The reassurance from his prescence dissipates the longer he reviews my answers. I place Armcoe above Boon and Chen under that, compiling the forms alphabetically the best I can.

"The question, *what anxieties do you experience on a day-to-day basis?* That's what it says—*ask about the girl in—*"

"I can't explain it." I cut him off. "I didn't write it."

He laughs an exhale from his nose and trades my form for another.

"Why did you come here anyway?" I ask him, starting a separate pile for Trentwith and Salinski.

"I thought you were full of shit and stealing from Alexis."

I look up at him but his face is covered with someone else's form. He starts tapping his foot many taps per second.

"Seriously?"

"Yeah."

I fall back in the chair. Nothing but black skies out the window, silence in the halls.

"Surely I couldn't't've imagined seeing his name on a form in here."

"Sure you could. Your mind plays tricks on you all the time."

The ticking clock says *get out*. The motion of his foot says *get out*. I want to pedal. Fast.

"Listen to this one," he says. "Waking hours are like reconnaissance missions with no real goal at the end. An effort in instant gratification. Everything imperative until I get there. Then I get there and need to get somewhere else. This goes on all day until I pass out somewhere. Nothing ever satisfies."

I put Tran above Trentwith and Seiger under Salinski.

"Is it going to make you feel better?" he asks. "Knowing all the details?"

He's still reading, but the foot tapping has stopped and the question echoes at least four times. Nothing in the office helps me find a suitable response. The baby glares at me, offering no clarity at all.

"Probably not," I tell him, unable to work out if Y comes before W. "I keep thinking about it though."

"You're not responsible for anyone else's decisions."

"I know that. But it's not like I never noticed him. I noticed him. I should've asked him. I didn't ask him. I could've helped him."

He swivels tiny swivels, face still hidden, head turning left to right as he scans the answers. The form catches the same sort of sigh The Dope Haus members reserve for the hopeless Casanova when he's being too emphatic.

"Hey, what does it say on that Post-it note? The one one the screen?"

"Doesn't say anything."

"What—it's blank?"

"No, there's a drawing of a key on it. See."

He unsticks it to show me; a circle, a line and two little lines. A key. The walls get even closer. I collate the rest of the pages, alphabetical or not.

"Doesn't it exhaust you, asking all these questions?"

Yes. I'm running on fumes.

I sigh and pick up the top form, but the words just blur.

"Absolutely, but they still exist."

He flips a page over the corner staple, turning so he's side on now. He holds a questionnaire a few feet infront of him, swallows loud and clears his throat.

"I'll tell you this because you're a stranger, and because I'll probably never see you again after this, but when I was a kid I was obsessed with space, I'd watch shows that displayed this divide; a blanket of dark blue separating me from the rest of universe and I thought that one day I'd be able to blast through it. Clearly I'm no astronaut, and obviously I haven't seen it for myself, but that idea just doesn't make sense anymore. There is no separation, no localization. How can there be? It's all connected; all of it. Every seemingly inconsequential decision, the way you cross the street, how you greet a stranger, the turns you take—they all matter, and if you begin to cross-reference them, you start to see the fabric of it all, and if you shut up for a bit, you begin to see how important you are in it."

He holds the form out across the desk, inviting me to grab it.

"Read the answer to question eleven."

I thought he already had, but there's only two lines of writing on the whole page. The rest of it is bright white, so bright it's almost purple. The letters blur from the chlorine, from the failed mission, from the longest day. I adjust, honing in on the words.

I DREAM OF HOME AT NIGHT AND FEEL PAIN IN MY CHEST FOR ALL THE LOVELY PEOPLE.

"Kills you a bit, doesn't it? Now look who wrote it." I flip back to the front page and learn Alexis's full name.

Part Two

THE SLIPPERY SLOPE

PAPER NAPKINS

I'm in a wind tunnel floating toward a fertile island at either sunrise or sunset. Gradients of purple, pink and orange, delete all traces of blue, and silhouettes of palm trees adorn the dock. The boat is completely still. A steady calm. Burning toast blows in on a breeze, shifting the jewels on the rim of the red chiffon lantern, exciting my hair so the ends dance gently over my face.

A quarter-turn reveals the drool patch I've created and through the weave of my lashes, the rest of the eatery emerges; a cup of water that I might've ordered, a steaming coffee I definitely did not, and a small family—in participants, not in stature—sitting in the booth by the window. Parental figures and a little girl all backlit by the morning sun.

She must've felt my gaze, the girl, because she changes from side profile to front profile, pausing her napkin throwing routine while purple blobs morph over her face. When her facial features emerge, I smile at her. She doesn't smile back, not in a mean way, more like she couldn't trust the offering. She looks about nine.

A waitress with a long dark ponytail and arrives at their table to drop off their meals—toast for the girl and different egg and bread arrangements for the adults. The girl resumes her napkin throwing routine over her plate.

"See what I did, ma?" The napkin rests in the palm of her hand.

"Eat your toast, honey."

"Look, I tied it up double and then I opened it here and made a little basket. See how when you scrunch it up it comes down quickly."

She throws it up and misses the catch. It lands on her toast then she flattens it out and throws it up again. "And look, when it's open it comes down slow."

Her observations are correct and she catches it this time. It's only when the bell over the door rings and a newcomer enters that she pauses to investigate. This guy is thirty-ish, tanned, bald head with an significant nose leading the way; it's angular and shark-like—perfect for swimming. He walks to the counter and leans over it like he's telling Long Ponytail a secret.

"Hayley, stop throwing that." Her mother speaks around a mouth full of toast. Hayley's not concerned by the request, more interested in her discovery.

"These eggs are delicious," her partner says.

"Mmm. I agree."

A breeze floats through the back door, and I swear, the palm trees sway accordingly.

◇

The second time I wake the sunset mural doesn't fool me. Hayley's gone, but remnants of their breakfast validates their existence. The coffee on the table in front of me is still full, though, no longer steaming. It must've been an act of charity from Ponytail. She's too busy tending to the hotplate to register my silent appreciation.

Sharkface sits close, far too close considering the ratio of empty chairs to occupied ones. He's on the couch on the brink of the wind tunnel adjacent to me. His bald head reflects a pink glow originating from the neon coffee cup on the wall next to the menu and on his left armrest, closest to my head, is his coffee cup, precariously positioned. Between his face and knees is a newspaper, wide open like it's about to swallow him whole.

It doesn't take long before the rustling of pages start to irk me, and the way he *tsks* at every page has me wondering why he endures the process at all. It's firing up internally, immensely. Little ballbearings in my groin and armpits start bounding off each other, prompting me to move, but I'm weighed down. Indolent.

"Thinking about your childhood?" he asks.

It's unlikely he's started reading out loud, so I check and see. His eyes are still on the paper but he shoots me a sideways glance so I know he's talking to me. I guess from his position he couldn't tell that the last thing I want to do this early was discuss my childhood, or anything else for that matter, when a perfectly serene wind tunnel was available.

Run, just run.

Go.

Get out.

He turns the page and the pink glow moves over the terrain of his creased forehead. All I see is sheen.

"I've been thinking about mine a lot lately." He leans in closer. "I have this theory, you want to hear it?"

Typically I have zero qualms about running away in the middle of a conversation like this, harbouring no concerns about the impression I would leave in my wake, but I find myself nodding along, hoping his is not going to be a long-winded theorem. Ponytail offers an apologetic look from behind the register, so I tell her thank you for the coffee. She responds by turning to greet a young couple who've just walked in arm in arm. Sharkface shakes the paper again.

"My life—my whole existence—is akin to this newspaper."

He waits for me to prompt him to go on. I don't, but he's ok with that. He opens the paper wider and tilts it in my direction.

"Let's say the average weekday-er is made up of forty percent bad news; all this injustice, corruption, greed, tales of infidelity and so on. Stories that are so, so important on the day, then tomorrow there's more, right?"

My handlebar shoulders have completely seized up to the point that nodding isn't an option. Ball-bearings frozen still, apprehensive about what's coming next.

"Then there are the advertisements. Huge ads with all the beautiful women."

Sharkface lets go of the left side of the paper so he can point to this woman in a bikini standing next to a red four-wheel drive. He flicks her in the stomach.

"Same as yesterday, same as last month, different pictures, different words but ultimately—the same. Doesn't even make sense. Does that make any sense to you?"

His question is presented rhetorically. I momentarily consider explaining the psychology behind the marketing strategy but that'd prolong the theory. He scans the page like he's reading lines.

"Let's make ads forty percent. Actually, forty five percent. I think that's more accurate. Forty-five percent for ads. So that's eighty-five percent, right?"

He checks with me that his calculations are correct and then continues.

"Then there's the masthead, the page numbers, all the by-lines and such, which would be akin to my name, my birthday, my father's name, etcetera—five percent, tops. Another five percent for the obituaries and classifieds; my getting petrol and paying bills and what not. "

He looks at me; the whites around his eyes increase.

"And you know what the sad part is?"

I open my palms to the heavens for assistance, and for a means of escape.

"All that's left are the good news stories. The ones we cut out and put up on our fridge. But soon they start to yellow. They dry out, tainted by exposure to the very air we breathe, and soon the paper loses its integrity and starts to flake away.

Lost forever."

Sharkface's pupils are a tiny speck of black, piercing into mine, willing me to agre, but I'm sinking. The sea is no longer still. My insides move in a figure eight motion and I'm about ready to jump over the edge.

Shit man.

He flicks the paper again.

"Dang—forgot sports. I'll have to recalculate the whole of it to accomodate Sumner's ego alone."

Sharkface closes the paper and tries for another sip of coffee but it's long finished. The cup echoes empty as it hits the armrest. He looks to me for feedback.

"Why do you read it then?" I ask him.

His expression is what I'd imagine it'd look like if someone knew a mute for many years, and then that mute spoke for the first time. His eyebrows rise in surprise, then descend in offense so his eyes are slivers. He folds the paper onto itself.

"You gotta keep up with what's going on in the world. It's better to know than to be ignorant."

"Aren't you consuming other peoples ignorance though? And biases?"

"I read it, then I know it. You can't keep your head in the sand."

"But what if it *is* the sand? How do you know what you think you know? "

He studies my questions for a moment but decides better of answering them, capping his decision with a laugh. The sudden movement must've caused his copius liquid consumption to catch up with him, because he asks me to save his seat while he goes to the bathroom.

I figure the chances of both our seats being occupied by the time he'd finished excreting were slim—and mine had the added benefit of a cool breeze—so when the door closes and the little sign changes from VACANT to ENGAGED, I stand up like a tree and leave.

ENHANCED

Selby's fifteen minutes late and I'm starting to look and feel a bit sad which isn't the kind of welcome students want to see upon entry to the on-campus eatery where it's 'pay-what-you-can'. People move with purpose. The side effects of over-loaded backpacks lend a certain lean to the flow. Through the masses this young guy with an eyebrow piercing does well to distract me; he's floating along the corridor like his brain's about four feet above his body. Eyes barely open, big smile on his face. He's pissed drunk.

For an extended duration this guy stands in the middle of the corridor, unsure about whether he wants to go into the men's room or not. He's standing there weighing up his needs, unconcerned about the groups who have to detour around him, completely oblivious to their inconvenience. Eventually he decides he can wait, and flops down on a couch opposite a gothic guy. He pauses typing to analyse the intruder and they look at each other briefly but neither of them say anything. Drunk guy starts experimenting with different sitting positions and gothic guy watches him with a look of disgust. Soon he decides it's impossible to continue his computer work with such an unsettled distraction, so he gets up and walks heavy down the corridor with his laptop still open at his chest. He must've been so hot in that thick coat.

Two people replace gothic guy on the couch; a guy and girl. They seem to be friends of drunk guy who are more aminable to his state. He goes on to tell them that he got paid fifty bucks to drink a bunch of beers in Nielsen Hall. These two are not overly surprised with this information until he tells them it happened in a controlled laboratory environment. His exact words were, *for science brah. For fucking sci-yence.* This detail spikes their interest, mine too. About fifteen minutes later, my inner compass guides me to Nielsen Hall and I'm up the stairs, down the corridor and sitting in a simple room containing dull blue carpet, four chairs and a man named Rasmus.

Rasmus is as blonde and fair as his name suggests. He is nowhere near as dull as Leonardo and much less judgmental about my prior indiscretions. After I fill out the release form, he delivers me a beer while I fill out a questionnaire about my leisure habits. He tells me to take my time so I put extra special effort into colouring in the circles to the neatest of my ability. He rewards my efforts with a second beer and to thank him, I draw a picture of a man in high shorts and suspenders which I'm sure he'll appreciate later, because for now, he's introducing me to three other people—Vladimir, Christian and Zamir.

"You guys get aquatinted and I'll be back in a minute with refills."

Rasmus leaves the room and the three of them occupy the other seats. I can't tell if they're pre-existing friends but it seems like they might entertain the idea post-experiment. Christian looks as though he's fresh to university judging on his size which is all I know about him so far. Vladimir is buff with a tight navy shirt and Zamir looks like a vertically stretched version of Jimmy.

They acknowledge me with a nod but not much more because Christian is mid-story.

"And then I said, *listen Jodie, I'll put these on the shelf because I want to, not because you're telling me to. Treat me like a subordinate and I will behave like one*."

"You didn't say that," Vladimir chides.

"No, of course not. I thought it though." Christian turns to me. "I would explain the context, but it'd take too long."

"It's really not a problem." I tell him.

"Are you a student here?" Zamir asks.

"No. Unless we're supposed to be to get paid for this?"

Before anyone answers Rasmus returns looking quite pleased with himself. He gives us each another beer, a half-pint this time. He stays in the room and we all cheers. Christian spills half of his beer on the carpet, so he downs the remnants in one gulp to maintain his buzz. I'm feeling too bubbled up to ask Rasmus what his mission is, so I store the question for later and excuse myself to the ladies.

Head spins ovals. Long, short. Long, short.

Over the tiled floor scenes of Selby waiting for me intersperse with visions of Rachel being informed by security that her office is now a crime scene. Those little white dots gravitate between episodes and I feel like *I'm* the glass holding the beer.

After a stablizing facewash I exit the bathroom to find them all standing in the corridor like I've been gone for a significant duration. Rasmus holds out a bottle of water to me—one point five litres—and suggests the five of us sit on the foothill by the university museum so we can sober up. The finality of his tone has me wondering whether the experiment is still underway, but I don't question him about it.

So much stimuli all at once.

Students weave at varying speeds.

Frisbee launched, frisbee caught.

Sun beats down. Colour in my cheeks.

Rasmus doesn't take notes but he's watching us all attentively. Not in a creepy way, more like in a concerned-facilitator-kind-of-way. He's listening to Vladimir paraphrasing this interview about the drummer from Express—Orion someone. He's saying Orion said how important it is to keep dreams silent so they don't get diffused by popular opinion. Something about how the house's framework always looks shit but there's a vision and the guy making the house can't let anyone else's lack of vision compromise his vision. It all makes a lot of sense but I don't say so. Instead, I preoccupy myself with the sun shards, tipping my head back toward to see what it'd look like if the whole world were inverted. People seemed to have an easy time adjusting. They look happy as ever.

Their conversation falls back a level and the details of the campus come to the fore.

Clocktower is faulty. Moves in five minute intervals.

Frisbee lowering, frisbee caught.

Christian leaves. Zamir does too.

I must've fallen asleep, but not enough to see black, just enough to stop thinking, because Rasmus and Vladimir become silhouettes, leering over me red and black and ten times taller than me from this angle. Vlad's got his hand out, saying something about coffee. Rasmus gives us our money and waves goodbye.

Every few steps Vlad asks me a question about myself. Answers are hard to come by. It's exactly like how Amina described her encounter with the rapper, but it's me with the glazed eyes. I remind myself to tell her that perhaps the rapper was extremely sensitive to alcohol the time he took her out, and his lack of follow up had nothing to do with how she acted or the answers she gave. He probably had a lot going on, or not much at all.

Vladimir looks relieved when I tell him I don't really like coffee. Some of his friends arrive at the perfect moment for him to join their flow, leaving me to consider how to spend this secret pocket of day that comes after a brief period of unconsciousness.

INDIGNANT

Four blocks until from home and sweat's collecting in my shirt pores, my heart's pulsing behind my ears. I'm pedalling fast. The white dots circulate and horns blast intense. I'm busting out of my skin and that's before I even notice the pair of mud-covered shoes toe-down on the concrete on other side of Pascal's Boulangerie. Momentum exposes the rest of him before I can decide whether or not I'm in the right state to see a dead body.

He's a man of about fifty—or a long drunk thirty-nine—and he's out cold. His right cheek presses into the concrete while a fly dances on his dehydrated bottom lip like maybe he ingested a tablespoon of salt before sleepin, but more likely though, was that he'd been on a bender which probably involved gambling because there's a seven of hearts wedged in the green trim of his trilby.

A brass bell rings as I enter Pascal's and I'm surrounded by an assortment of golden baked goods. It smells like butter and warmth and Sundays. Over the glass counter behind an excess of facial hair is a baker awaiting my request, his mood as dull as grey. Had I been a purchasing customer, I might've rethought my hunger for fear of contamination.

"There's a man passed out outside and I'm pretty sure he's in the process of decomposing. Could we give him a cup of water?"

Beardy shakes his head and continues wrapping this tea-towel around his palms. "Not allowed to give out tap water to customers. Health codes."

"It can't be too good for business having a corpse outside your shop."

He's standing firm amongst soft brioches' and I'm asking him silently if he's serious. He answers *yes* by not saying a thing and I've got no response because I'm busy searching for his logic. Then he unravels one hand and points toward the drinks fridge. Bottles of water line the top shelf. I get his hint, and although the issue is pressing and his gross attitude is watching, I linger for a brief moment at the open door, relishing the coolness emanating from the vents. It's total heaven. Then, because the issue *is* pressing, I grab the cheapest water bottle and head for the door.

"You need to pay for that."

It's like we haven't talked at all.

"Did you not hear what I said? Guy? Outside? Shrivelled?"

"Not my problem."

The bell chimes again, like it's trying to wake me from this civil nightmare. A round man in slacks grazes my arm on his way to the counter and starts requesting a succession of desserts. Beardy is at his service. The next thing I know is everything is blurry around the edges and a pistachio croissant is decompressing on the floor next to my right foot.

My right palm shines with buttery grease.

Beardy is fuming and Fat Slacks isn't enjoying the interruption either. I'm out the door before the scenario catches up with me and blinding light bounces off the windscreen of a cop car slowing to a halt next to the problemed gambler. As they step onto the curb I centre and mount my bike, and behind me the bell chimes again and Beardy is yelling out profanities. A car door slams. I don't look back. I'd fall if I did. Fences blur into brown, into speed. Cars appear from nowhere. Cyclists too.

Quads tense, knees lock.

I merge into a bike lane, surrounded by cyclists, thinking I'm safe when this lady with two shopping bags by her side pulls out right in front of me looking at me like *I'm* the crazy person who just introduced myself to road traffic. She goes left, I go left. I go right, she does too. Our synchronicity makes her so angry that she stops dead still, lifts her face to the sky and waits there in the middle of the bike lane for *me* to manoeuvre around *her*. I do exactly that, wondering which store I could go in to by her the three seconds of her life she just lost, certain she'd take the time to go in there with me.

Fucks sake—red light.

A lycra-clad shield forms around me, guarding me left, right and back.

Can't serve tap water to customers. Do I look like a fucking health inspector?

This guy next to me, about nineteen with a tiny ponytail and black studs in his ears, looks me up and down and says, "No, not at all."

It's then I remember I have fifty bucks in my back pocket.

NO QUESTIONS, NO ANSWERS

I can't hear a single bird. They've vacated the vicinity and it's not particularly comforting. Neil must've noticed my concern because he stops after four laps, removing his goggles to reveal two red oval indents framing his silver eyes. Pool dew hangs onto his steel wool eyebrows.

"How's life treating you, young lady?"

I consider his question as I emulate his position holding the metal bar under the lane block. This enables me to use him as a human shield from the sun's glare.

In my head it goes like this:

Well, Neil, it seems that I'm displaying behaviour akin to someone on hard, hallucinogenic drugs. Also, I'm waiting for a sign, a small or a big one, that will set me on the right course. In the meantime, I can't suppose I'll find the answers I need from other people, but at the same time, I know my view is extremely narrow and some people have exactly the answers I need. I'm also wondering about the validity of nouns, about my childhood and whether the movements I'm making are in vain.

"I don't really know how to explain it," I tell him.

"Wouldn't worry about it on a day like today," he says. "S'gonna be stormy this afternoon. Rain'll make it better. Always does."

The sky is practically cloudless; wisps of white on different levels. Lower ones move fast while the higher ones are perfectly still and the rest is so blue it glimmers green around the edges. I silently counter his forecast while he watches a lady in a rice-picking hat kneeling near some tomatoes on the other side of the fence in the community garden. She's got a mini spade in hand. Something about the way she's flicking dirt over her shoulder causes Neil's cheekbones to rise. It makes me wonder if I spent more time in the pool, perhaps the space between my eye corners and hairline would be as naturally vacant as his. Right now mine feel like a thousand sacks of sand piled one on top of the next, condensed to a size that fits the area, then locked in a vault and freeze dried for extra measure.

"Can't see it yet, but it's coming," he says. "Can tell by the birds."

Again, no birds. All I can hear is a distant siren and a truck moving with glass bottles in the back. I'm trying to tune in; beyond the swipe of cars, the kids calls, and the sounds of an excavator when this high-pitched whistle blasts like whoever dealt it sensed my vulnerable state.

Heads turn to see what's happening. A woman screams. Teen Lifeguard's mid-flight, angled straight as a line toward this black wet of hair, floating inanimate in the open section. Flailing limbs move toward her and at the edge of the pool, this woman—the mother, I assume— trips over her sarong and lands smack on her knees without her arms to break her fall. Her face is pure terror like the impact has shattered her heart.

Teen Lifeguard's at the ladder with this limp girl under his arm. Her black hair is everywhere making it hard to tell which way is her front. Her body's floppy, dripping.

Two Neil look-a-likes help hoist the girl on the pavers; her wrists, ankles, neck—so loose. Another woman is struggling to lift the mother to her feet; she's so hysterical she can't stand, clambering forward and fighting off arms.

Neil's up the ladder and between his hairy legs and the dripping bodies, Teen

Lifeguard's back muscles clench and release with every press on the girl's chest. She moves boneless while her mother dangles just as loose in the arms of strangers; completely wasted and hopelessly watching. Bystanders hold their mouths. The older kids run up to see.

Limp-gut runs from the office with haste in his uneven strides. As he arrives, a stream of water spurts up out of the girl's mouth and she's coughing, contorting on her side. Teen Lifeguard falls backwards out of the resuscitation circle with his knees to the sky and his head hanging between them. He's holding his left wrist with his right hand, surging forward and back like he might puke.

Neil's right up next to him, hand on the middle of his back. The kid doesn't seem to acknowledge the touch. It might be the chlorine, but from here it looks like he's shaking, drips streaming to the concrete from the tip of his wet fringe.

The crowd disperses, the girl coughs more, the mother cries and sirens sound louder.

I wondered if Neil was getting my message that that was probably the perfect way to explain it.

WALSH-BENNETT LAB #2

I guess because it's one AM and I'm a girl, they have to get a girl assistant because there's a dark room involved and we're alone for several minutes. Sandra looks tired but speaks with patience and precision. I get the impression she's enjoying the effects of varied sleep patterns and the rewards of commitment to a task. A task which requires no questionnaire thus far.

"Before you say anything Louise, it's best you don't speak," Sandra tells me the good news as she fills a plastic tray with various pieces of equipment.

"What's going to happen is this: we're going to put these two electrodes on your forehead, near your temples. Another two below your collarbone, and one on each wrist. We're also gonna clip this little guy here on your right middle finger, is that cool with you?"

I nod and she puts the pulse oximeter on my middle finger. She then wipes my right temple with a sanitary wipe and presses on an electrode. Same for the left.

"Cool, then you'll sit in our make-shift cinema through that door over there and you'll watch a five-minute movie. About fifteen minutes later, the same movie plays again, but we need you to sit there the whole time, does that make sense?"

I nod again and she attaches the electrodes to my collarbone and wrists.

"Anything you're cautious about?"

I shake my head. She nods. After triple checking the integrity of all the electrodes, she ushers me up and leads me through the door.

The room is cool and dark with curtained walls. A luxurious white chaise is positioned in the centre of the room facing a big screen TV mounted to the wall. I assume the seat is for me, so I get comfortable while Sandra tends to a computer behind me.

"Doesn't matter if you fall asleep, that's pretty normal at this hour. You'll be by yourself during that fifteen minute break, then after the second showing we'll chime a bell three times to indicate we're coming back in. The bells aren't loud so you won't be alarmed, but you will notice them."

I'm wondering what happens if I don't notice them when she comes to my side, holding out a clipboard.

"The envelope is for you—your compensation. I'm giving it to you now because it's best if you refrain from speaking for as long as possible after we've finished. Inside the envelope you'll also find a questionnaire and a reply paid envelope. If you could fill it in tomorrow and send it back within the week, that'd be great. Now I just need you to sign this release down the bottom there."

I can barely see anything in the light.

"Should I read it?"

She shrugs. "You can. Basically says that we're not responsible if anything happens to you on the way home. Precautionary because of the late hour."

I sign on the dotted line and she takes the clipboard from me.

"So this is where I say thanks. Thanks Louise. You're all set to go."

Sandra disappears behind me, presses some buttons and then the door seals shut behind her. Shortly after, the screen comes on, black at first, then a radar graphic begins a count down from four.

The movie is in black and white. Sporadic flashes of dust cross the screen and burn marks appear in the corners occasionally, like it's been doctored to appear older than it really is. The basic premise is this guy—about fifty—who is also in a cinema, but the old fashioned kind with curved rows and ornate gold trimmings. On his screen is a movie playing scenes of warfare. Tanks and soldiers lined up one after the other, moving in uniform. This guy is standing in the space between the screen and the first row of seats and he's trying to pick up this massive remote control. Massive meaning it's about seven foot long and clearly made of foam, but because it's so big, he keeps fumbling over it in a Three Stooges-kind-of-way. The more he tries, the more his energy depletes. After much futile effort, he stops trying, turns his back to the screen and looks down at the floor. At the exact moment he looks away, the film cuts to this romance scene where a man and a woman are standing on a balcony while a breeze lifts her silk scarf over the man's face which must've smelt amazing to him because he looks orgasmic. Of course. the guy doesn't see this part because he's got his back to the screen. After a passionate exchange between the couple, he looks up again and as soon as he does, the screen cuts to footage of a memorial service. He's still for a moment, looking up at the screen, then he bolts up the cinema stairs and out of frame so it's just the memorial service playing, then his screen goes black and after about thirty seconds, my screen goes black too and says 'FIN".

By the end of the second showing I'm too tired to bother asking Sandra whether I was in the negative stimuli control group and not the positive and peaceful one the guy who lives on Stranton must've been exposed to. I'm also too tired to bother asking her why it's described as 'audio-sensory' when the movie is silent and I'm told not to talk, but when she comes in after the bells chime, she's got this tight-lipped smile happening, so I check my pocket for the envelope and smile the same smile goodbye.

ZENITH

At first I thought the pool filter might need servicing, but then I notice the clear tube connecting Moongoggle's nostrils to what looked like a camera bag. I soon realise they've modernised oxygen tanks since the last time I saw one. It gives off this squirt of deliberate air every other heartbeat which causes his chest to rise and his to scar glisten.

He's wearing swim briefs tonight, this morning, this moon. Green like the dark green from a pack of colouring pencils. His hands look especially corrugated and he's got a new blood spot shaped like a heart where his bicep used to be. Arms are straight by his sides and his fingers are curl up, tapping the inside of his palm about a hundred times a minute. I do the same and it's really hard work.

Through his goggles he must've noticed me mimicking him because his chin-skin folds on itself when he turns to me as I sit on the other moon-chair. I feel bad to think he might think I'm mimicking him, so I silently tell him I'm only trying to understand his position. I can tell he understands—he's just got peace in his wrinkles.

As I'm settling in to a full recline, he's leans toward his tank like he's trying to get away. I'm up spotting him, in case he rolls off the chair and onto the pavers, but it's an overreaction on my part because he rolls back holding a strap of rubber connected to a mask with a snorkel attached. He shakes it a few times indicating I should take it off him.

"Try it," he says on a whisper. "You float."

ROUND #2

Rachel is not in a good way. From here it looks like she's consumed a six pack of coffee and maybe three lines of coke. She's pacing by the bike racks with her elbows wide, phone by one ear and papers scrunched up by the other one which makes her look as though she's trying to fly away. The midday sun casts shadows over her face and shine gleams over her forehead.

In light of her strained expression, the idea of breaching the topic of Owen's missing application doesn't seem so bright. She ends the call and pushes through the double doors, and I know it's probably the worst idea, but I follow her, not really sure whether I'm going to her office or not.

Between the third and fourth floor, this woman with blonde dreads descends, looking at me as if she's trying to match my face to some internal security footage from the late night escapade. I continue upward as if I'm in a hurry.

"Excuse me?" Dreads is waiting on the platform below. When I've cleared a reasonable head-start, I turn to see what she wants.

"Hmm?"

"Sorry, but were you in here a few months ago for the music perception experiment?"

Phewf.

"Possibly. Which one is that?"

"Yeah, it was you. I remember the way you tied your shoes."

I look down at my well-worn laces. "How's that?"

"Loosely. Aren't you worried they're going to fly off?

"Not really, no."

"First I'm going to smoke this smoke, but we've had a cancellation. There's a hundred bucks in it for you and a free hair wash if you're interested?"

"Why do you wash my hair?"

"We have to put this EEC goop on your head to attach the electrodes so we wash it afterwards, otherwise you'd be walking around all lubed-up."

Dreads presents a lucrative proposal. I take a minute to consider it while she studies my laces.

"I've got a meeting now, but something tells me it might not be happening. How about I come by your office when I know and if you're there, you're there."

"Simpatico." She salutes me then disappears around the corner. "Fifth floor, C-11."

Rachel's door is shut and I'm standing outside completely aware that I'm about to push my luck as far as it could go, but another possibility was that she'd understand and might be able to shed some light on the situation. I figure the worse she'd do is kick me out, and I'd go get my hair washed semi-professionally.

Rachel's collecting her personals when I enter. She's got a panic in her eye more pressing than a student loitering on campus after hours. At least, that's what I tell myself. My words are out before she says anything.

"I can come back."

"No need. Tanya's waiting for you in the lab. She's my assistant. She'll be doing the next section with you."

"Can I ask you something quickly?"

"I really can't right now Louise."

She zips her bag shut and ushers me out, pulling the door closed behind her.

◇

The second round is just as stifling, however the buffer of experience provides some comfort. Tanya's practised in her approach and exhibits genuine concern for my well-being, providing me water and small talk during the breaks. Claustrophobia reaches about an eight.

When it's over I sit on the other side of Tanya's desk while she types. She's got her eyes on the screen and she hits the keys like she's playing an instrument.

"Now, usually we'd pay you a part-payment today, but Rachel forgot to give it to me in her haste. I'll ask her about it when she's back in. Probably best to call first though. Want to see your results? They're super interesting."

Even though I'm white-knuckled from the inconvenience, I concede with a nod because she seems excited to share her findings. She rolls over to the printer and retrieves a page which she aligns next to an identical looking one, using a ruler to make sense of it all.

"Definite improvement this time round. Accuracy improved to sixty-eight percent."

"That's an improvement?"

"Most people do better the second time. I guess they know what they're in for."

She slides the ruler down the pages, nodding to herself, then reaches out to a mega set of headphones and extends them in my direction.

"Here, put these on. We overlay the first recording with the second. You can hear the difference."

"Oh no, that's ok. I don't need to hear myself."

"It's so interesting. You gotta hear it."

Tanya's thrusting the headphones insistently so I indulge her. Once they're positioned over my head she presses a button and this buzz sounds, then this voice says either '*head*' or '*hid*' — I really can't tell. The noises barely sound like words and it sure doesn't sound like me.

I take the headphones off immediately and hand them back to Tanya, figuring I'd indulged her plenty.

"Is that really what I sound like?"

"Yeah it is. Isn't it great?"

"You're telling me there's absolutely no difference between what I sound like here, sitting opposite you right now and what I sound like through these headphones."

"There really is no difference."

Yep. Indulged her plenty.

◇

Every back-street I turn down is either clogged with a garbage truck or contaminated with dry dust construction suggesting a detour that's always uphill. The harder I peddle, the tighter the rubber band pressure suffocates my airways. Handlebar shoulders engage to maximum.

Breathing is like eating a tea towel. Everywhere smells like a fresh packet of cigarettes; dry like chalk.

Nothing in, nothing out.

INERTIA

Dynamite spends a long moment deciding how he feels about our prior meeting before making any decisions about granting me access. He eventually does, without a word.

Aaron's sitting on the floor at the coffee table with his chin on his knee and a pen in his hand. He's happy to see me or just plain happy. Dynamite falls into the one-man couch, legs hanging over the edge, face to the ceiling.

"I think I left my phone here the other night," I tell them.

"Oh really?" Aaron looks around. "I haven't seen it. Have you seen it D?"

Dynamite shakes his head. "Maybe it's in Alexis room."

"Why would it be in Alexis room?" Aaron asks.

"It's as good a place as any."

Dynamite looks at me, silently telling me something I can't translate, then rearranges himself quickly, leaning forward toward the notepad in front of Aaron.

"Read that last part back?"

Aaron clears his throat and takes a moment to find the spot on the page.

"A slower precise effort will always exceed a medium paced, half-prepared effort which beats a fast and reckless effort, in regard to satisfaction."

I must've made some sort of sound because they both look at me, waiting.

"Is Alexis around?" I ask.

"He's in his room."

Aaron points in the direct of his room, then looks at Dynamite and slaps both his hands on his knees.

"You're right, you're absolutely right."

"Not really, but it's one school of thought." He holds out his hand. "Here, pass it here."

Aaron rips the sheet off the notepad and passes it over the coffee table.

"That's why I love Susan Boyle," Aaron says, as he sits back down. "Do you think she's happy?"

Dynamite considers the question as he folds the paper so the edges meet exactly.

"Depends how she is with inertia."

The only occupant of Alexis's room is the 2D white tiger who doesn't say much as I put the card back in the vase, finalising that failed mission. It feels like he's watching, this phantom version of him, laughing at me with his arms crossed over the thirteen. I don't stick around in case he starts talking.

I'm at the front door, stunted. Between me and it is a vision of me pushing my bike across their courtyard wishing I'd sat on the couch with them while they spoke about Susan Boyle like she's a friend of theirs.

Before I think otherwise, that's exactly what I do.

"He's not home," I say, sitting on the couch next to a puzzle box, preparing myself for a silent exchange of confusion to pass between them about my extended stay. Strangely, it doesn't eventuate. Instead, Aaron holds a black sketchbook out to me.

"Check out these Louise." He moves the puzzle box to sit next to me. "Ha. That rhymes — these Louise."

I flip open the cover to find a watercolour painting of three sharks with swords taped to their heads like bayonets.

"It's called Shark Fin Soup," Aaron says. "It's a sharks-eye-view of the boat people situation. Jarrad did them."

Dynamite stretches his arms overhead exposing his snail trail and bursting tension bubbles in one of his shoulders.

"You painted all these?"

He picks up the paper he'd just folded and starts tapping the corner against the table. "Yep."

"Don't just look at the pictures Louise, you gotta read it." Aaron turns a page for me. "It's about these sharks who are seeing all this displacement so they come in to help, but all these spears and javelins are spiralling in, and the barbed wire nets—those are the whaling ships, in case you didn't get that, so it's like *sushi-city*; the sharks efforts are hampered. But then Samurai's come and there's this huge battle to the sound of The Dell-tones—do you know The Dell-tones? and then like magic, everyone swaps shoes—you know, like they did post-war—right Jarrad?"

"Right." Dynamite's tapping faster, denting the corner of the paper.

"His first book was called Rapture. It's about Lady Di and self-doubt."

"Can I read that one?"

"No," Dynamite says. "It's nowhere near finished."

"Your first book? How many are there?"

"Fifteen," Aaron says for him.

"Fifteen? You're kidding?"

Dynamite's not kidding. He's not looking particularly comfortable with me holding his book either.

"What do you do with them?"

"What do you mean *what I do with them?* I do them, then I've done them."

"The illustrations are excellent. Do you sell them?"

Aaron shakes his head.

"Jarrad doesn't believe in selling art. He says some things aren't made for the market. He says the real art is the mystery under the rag and goes unnoticed 'til the artist is dead which is probably about the time he, and the world, is ready for it."

"*He* can talk for himself," Dynamite interupts.

"Sorry," Aaron turns another page. "I get excited."

I flip another page which is a close up of a shark's eye; black and shiny with a reflection of a girl falling with a harpoon through her gut. Two bubbles above her. Even without reading it, it all makes perfect sense from where I'm sitting.

"Oh wait."

Aaron looks at the letter between Dynamite's fingers and moves over to swipe it from him. He sits back down at the table and grabs the pen.

"What was that thing you said... the mundane something?"

"I can't remember now."

"Something about how the mundane is the poetry we seek? Yes, that's it. That's exactly it."

Aaron unfolds the page, shaking his head in genuine admiration.

"Nah don't write that, it sounds wrong now," Dynamite says.

"Too late. Oh fuck." Aaron's head goes back like he's just been shot in the chest. Dynamite leans over the letter to inspect the problem.

"What?"

"Won't fit. No matter. I'll start again and write smaller this time. Won't take long."

"No, leave it like that. I like hyphenations. Shows optimism."

Aaron looks at me and sits up straight.

"We're writing a letter to that playwright."

"Harris Parchment?"

"Yeah," Dynamite says. "Him."

"It's a commentary on his commentary. We have some questions to his questions."

"Is it going to make you feel better?" I ask him. "Knowing all the details?"

Dynamite looks at me like, *did you really just say that?* So I look back at him like, *yes, I did. So is it?*

He doesn't respond.

I close Shark Fin Soup and put it on the table.

"I could deliver that for you." I motion toward the letter.

"Oh, that's okay." Aaron looks over letter proudly and refolds it according to the creases. "We'll get Alexis to give to him."

Dynamite stands abruptly and throws his pen on the table which makes Aaron jump, then laugh at himself.

"I have hunger. You coming?"

"Where are you going?"

"Where do you think?"

"A-lex-ee," Aaron calls out. "We're going to get a fa-la-fel."

"He's not home," I tell them. Aaron looks at me and loses his smile. He turns to Dynamite. "That's three nights running."

Dynamite shakes his head a few small shakes and withdraws his wallet from his back pocket. He's disappointed with the contents of the cash compartment.

"You got any money?"

"I got money," Aaron sings. "I got more money than the bank can hold."

"Are you sure I can't deliver that for you? I don't have a single thing to do today."

Aaron looks at Dynamite for confirmation who looks at me briefly, shrugs, puts his wallet back in his pocket and heads toward the front door. Aaron slides the letter in a replied paid envelope, crosses out the pre-typed details and marks it 'H. Parchment'.

"You coming?" Dynamite calls from down the hall. Aaron seals the envelope and hands it to me.

"You can't miss his place. He lives in Westwood. It's the building as soon as you exit the south metro exit. Looks like the Leaning Tower of Pizza."

"I'll leave it in his mailbox—then it can be anonymous too."

He smiles widely.

"Excellent, excellent idea. Apartment 22."

◇

With three heaves to go before the peak of Range Valley Drive, catapults of rain land in my eyelashes, warping the road and smearing its ornaments. The house with the frangipani tree indicates the start of the short plateau which requires no pedalling; the last few metres before the descent to Westwood, before momentum takes over. Everything is still in anticipation; my shirt, my hair, my mind.

And I go.

I'm floating. Flying. Pedals spin on their own accord. Air bubbles my shirt. Hair whips manic as the wind blasts and my eyes glaze and the trees spread out at their peaks so there's no dividing line up above. Colours merge, I'm being moved. It's fresh, the dew in the air.

I'm carried. I'm light.

I'm too light.

The quake of the handlebars increases; my only warning.

No time for breaks. No time to redirect.

One blink to clear view.

Rear window. Teeth collide.

Noise escapes my ears, or my nose, or it doesn't escape at all, just circulates within.

I'm in inertia and I know it.

MAGIC TRICK

Barely ten steps in, everything shifts. What's left of the city racket falls to a hum like it can't penetrate the millions of leaves, moonlight shines on the last of the cobblestone path before the steps, and then the stirring begins; vibrations of frogs and crickets and tiny invisible insects mix with the crunch of gravel and the catapult of stones.

Stairs. Platform. Stairs. Platform.Stairs.

The black between each step is so black I can't look for too long.

Rubber soles flap. Weight's all in my toes.

Stairs. Platform. Gravel path—about about five cars wide. It's half moon-lit, half not. The canopy towers above me, so many fragrances it's dense to breathe in.

On my left through the mosiac of leaves, the city's thrown out like confetti, shimmering gold, appearing and disappearing depending on foliage density.

On my right, ancient trunks ascend and every now and then, shrieks from a well-drunk night filter down from a path above. Probably kids; maybe drunk, maybe happy and likely as repelled by my nervous energy as I am of their excitement.

Abyss up ahead. Through it, a glowing white shape is coming right at me.

I've veered to the right wondering if I should've worn white to stand out or black to disappear. I can't tell what colour I'm wearing. No pigments in this light.

Right toe finds the pointy end of a rock. Pain level: maximum, but I can't stop now.

Heavy breath.

Flap, rubber soles. Even the crickets, the frogs, and the insects have shut up.

Steps come quicker and the shape forms into a shirt—sleeveless. Legs—thin and muscular with softened skin around his knees. He's got elastics connecting his wrists to his ankles, and he's pumping biceps with every step. Cheeks go hollow, puffed, hollow, puffed. Breathing is heavy, but not heaving. He's in control.

"Baby, they're good," he would've said after that first climb all those years ago. It wasn't the resistance of the elastics that made him feel so invigorated that morning, more the accomplishment of the feat. The early rise, the chase into darkness. He felt so high that day he hasn't changed a thing about his route since. He does for his grandkids. That's what I imagine anyway.

Old man passes me, whispers of his steps.

One smell dominates—burnt wood chips.

The carcass lies in the recess. The sting of the cut lingers fresh. I wonder what the old man thought of it, whether he saw it leering, what he thought of the smell.

Up ahead, more abyss. Always the same distance away.

Flap, rubber sole.

Flap, rubber sole.

The smell fades to fresh again and city lights glimmer on the left once more, glinting in tune with the frogs and the crickets and the bugs and the insects who're making up for their quiet moments. Frames change according to blink frequency; quick—then slow to open. Blurry—then stretching spears.

It's not until I'm right next to them that I see them—the moon-blue steps. I'm taking them, and I'm taking them barefoot.

Stairs. Platform. Stairs.

A runner passes me, ease in his movement. Halfway comes quick but so does fatigue. Certain sections of Westwood light up through the tree tops, spaced out and far away, while silhouettes move around on the look-out, the nightcap to a memorable night. Above and to the right, the drunken calls carry louder, providing the fuel I need for the last leg—the jurassic gravel incline.

It's handlebar everything. It feels like my head has already plateaued and is waiting for the rest of me to catch-up. Quads burn, weight all in my toes.

When I reach level ground a breeze rewards my efforts and I discover my shirt's burgundy mixed with a blue haze coming from the east. Blue and green melt together and a golden gleam of the imminent sunrise enlivens the mountains like water's reflecting on them.

It's still mostly dark on the west side, so I take the back way by the tiered flower boxes, filled with blooms still sleeping, like the two men on the benches with brown paper bottles by their sides. The flags whip, no pigments up there.

I sit atop the balustrade, watching the congregations at the apex. Someone laughs too loud for this scene. A girl jumps into a man's arms wrapping her legs around his waist. A hooded guy walks atop the balustrade while neighbouring clusters pause to watch, likely hoping they hadn't ventured so far only to witness tragedy.

Male voices drift up through the scrub below and behind me. Their mission more verbal than my last six days combined.

"What do you think the darkest place on earth is?"

"Under the sea, of course."

The number '13' glows through the thin trunks and shortly after, Alexis's nearly bald head emerges, along with the rest of him. Three others follow, not including Dynamite, nor Aaron. The last one to emerge is a well-drunk Harris

Parchment. He's trailing like there's a slack string connecting him to the rest of them, lurching in bursts when it gets tight enough.

"It's all relative, isn't it?" he says. "Dark's not dark to an owl."

No-one replies because they're already at the apex and no longer listening. Alexis is looking toward the sunrise like he's the captain, and the city's his sea while Harris turns circles with his face to the sky. He's turning too fast like he's about to twist himself seperate, then falls to his knees like the lady at the pool. I feel it all through my groin and hips, the space shocked and echoing. He slaps the pavers with both hands, laughing like it's told a good joke.

"You got me, didn't you?" he says. "You really got me."

Alexis backtracks and helps him up. It takes Harris a moment to recalibrate.

"Go backwards once, that'll even you out."

The advice comes from the smaller one of the other two and Harris believes it to be sage wisdom. He turns fast in the not-backwards direction, then tries to run forward. Again—he's floored. He's laughing, but it's not good. The sound was not good. Alexis doesn't help him up this time. I feel like he feels as sick as I do.

Turns out, enough focus on a person brings about a certain energetic pull. Alexis engages zoom and extends his head toward me like an old man trying to read the paper without glasses. His wave is the question, so I wave back *yes* and he puts his hands in his pockets and starts gliding my way.

City lights blur behind him the closer he gets, and the closer he gets, the puffier his face looks.

"Louise? S'that you?"

I nod one significant nod and start rubbing my shins as if I'm cold but I'm not, while he sits on the ledge at my feet, facing inward and surveying the drop behind him which I measured it when I sat down and deemed that I'd probably survive if I maintained full awareness during the fall.

Alexis' eyes are swollen like he's had some sort of allergic reaction. He pushes his index finger into my shin bone.

"Are you illusory Lou? I can't tell."

I nod, and he notices the state of my chin.

"Oh shit—what happened to you?"

My shrug conveys it's unexplainable and my raised eyebrows confirms what I think he already knows. He peers in closer to inspect the red line coursing down the centre of my neck so I lift my chin to show him the full extent of the cut. He squints confused, then smiles to diffuse it.

"Not much for talking, huh?" He leans back about five degrees. "That's cool. I hear ya."

We both turn our attention to Harris then, who is sitting cross-legged by himself with his back to the lookout. He's tracing circles around him like he's creating a safety zone. Graceful as described, but he wasn't there at all. Even if I still had the letter, I feel like he'd drop it off the ledge just to see how it lands.

He notices me thinking about him and pushes himself up, then starts heading our way.

"S-Y-Z-Y-G-Y." He sings. "It's you again. Well I'll be."

He leans against the balustrade on the other side of Alexis with his hands in his pocket and his eyes on the horizon. His face is all puffed up too. It's like they've both slept face down on blocked nose after not drinking water for a week. Harris looks at the drop behind him, then puts a smoke in his mouth and juts his chin toward the other side of the apex.

"Look at that display," He searches his pockets for a lighter. "Who has the internal capacity for that shit?"

"What shit?" Alexis's voice is tired, over it.

"See, this is the thing..." he says around the smoke. "I can see how and why family members stay together through the years, but can't see what it is a man and a woman remain attached for, outside of security concerns."

"How do you think families start?" Alexis asks him. Harris doesn't answer because he's looking across the apex trying to solve his own riddle.

"I've seen them broken, don't like it. Seen them working, don't like it."

"Have you ever *experienced* it working?" Alexis asks, then flash-glances down the drop to indicate that might be our best method of escape.

"I've experienced the rise and the subsequent, inevitable fall. It's equal enough."

Alexis rubs his hand over his jaw line. "I wouldn't think so."

It's then that Harris squints at Alexis, then at me like he's suspicious he's interrupting some pre-planned rendezvous. Smoke billows around his head.

"People will find the meaning in anything, whether it was intended or it wasn't. It's a wonder anyone can maintain any level of consistency in something so futile."

"People will also make sweeping generalisations that render themselves redundant." Alexis replies.

Harris laughs out some smoke. "That's all I do Lex. Or maybe it's the acid I took before. Yeah, you know what? I think it is."

He stubs out the smoke on the ledge after two puffs and puts the remnants in his chest pocket, patting it twice.

"You guys, right now, it's like the play was within a play and I'm in this other production hyper aware of where I am on the stage right now."

"Oh yeah?" Alexis asks. "So what's the next scene?"

"Well," Harris moves to stand infront of us. "You know the sailing they have in the Olympics? Those twelve-foot boats?"

He looks to each of us and Alexis nods so I nod too even though I didn't really know those specific boats. I could easily imagine a twelve-foot boat though.

"Well this one time, we were out off the coast of Guatemala, anchored in for the night, and the water, it's this is muddy brown, so dirty you can barely see your own reflection in it." He's looking beyond the concrete, imagining it.

"So it's night time, and we're anchored in, and the next day, when we wake up, the water is perfectly clear, so clear you can see every individual grain of sand on the ocean floor. Completely pristine."

Alexis looks relieved like perhaps he was expecting a different ending.

"How did that happen?" he asks.

"Cool breeze blew in from Antarctica and cleared it all up."

Alexis crosses his arms over his chest. Hands tucked under his armpits.

"So you're saying we're in for a cool change?"

"Indeed my friend. It can't stay this hot for too long. It always evens out."

"And what's syzygy?"

It takes Harris a moment to register the question.

"Syzygy? It's a pair of connected or corresponding things. Conjuction and opposition."

"Can you use it in a sentence?"

"Yes. Spell syzygy."

Harris winks at both of us and bows in farewell, then runs toward the other two, kicking off the balustrade when he arrives which doesn't get him very far at all. Alexis doesn't look like the captain anymore, more like a dyslexic student trying to understand an algorithm written in roman numerals.

"Louisa, can I ask you something?"

I try for a *yes* but only foreign sound cracks and the word doesn't transfer, though I'm sure he can see my nod in his periphery.

"Have you ever done a magic trick that didn't work out?"

I consider his question and he laughs at whatever expression I'm wearing.

"With some people, you get stuck in old habits, you know? They expect it of you, so you're already expecting it of yourself in a sense, and that means you're already halfway there unless you anticipate their expectation and decide to stand firm against it before it starts, you know? You need resolve. A strong conviction."

I wish I could redeliver his words about picking an answer that suits. Instead I watch as he leans back further over the drop, looking skyward.

"Some parties just don't get it that you have to go in with at least a small amount of believing, otherwise what they expect of you is useless and never works."

I definitely agree with that one and I think he can tell. He straightens up and smiles lovely cheekbones at me.

"I can't tell you much more than that. I'll speak in earnest and we all know that'll get a person nowhere."

PHENOMENON

It's mid-morning Saturday and I've neither applied the foresight or the strategy the weekend requires. I'm sitting on the twenty-fifth step squinting light circles over the park, not sure whether I'm coming or going. My efforts not to wake the house, I discover, are in vain when I see Selby approaching from Lincoln. She seems happy with the way her day is unfolding, or she did until she arrives on the twenty second step and her face contorts into a mixture of intrigue and empathic pain. Her bag drops to her feet and she kneels down in front of me, moving in for a better angle.

"Oh man! Look at your chin—it's like the bone is right there." Her finger hovers at a considered distance. "What happened to you?"

I try to air the word 'van' but there's no substance to the syllable. Her eyebrows shoot up. I clear my throat and force down a swallow. Maximum effort required.

"How did—" She abandons the inquiry while I push into my chin, feeling the feeling of it, bruised and tender, while telling her silently that *yes, I too was unaware that could even happen*. Selby purses her lips like it's all very funny, then leans back against the railing. Her eyes small, glistening and lively.

"So this is... interesting," she spaces out. "And it might actually eventuate into a very successful solution." She looks up at me. "Can you really not talk?"

I shrug and swallow.

"Huh."

I turn my palms to the sky for answers.

"You know Simon? Zac's friend Simon? Also known as DJ Simon?"

I turn my palms to my knees for fewer answers and start shaking my head. Once the shaking starts, it doesn't stop. Even the internal silent screams of NO rasp dry on my throat.

Oh god no.

"Seems you made quite an impression on him the way you disappeared from the show the other night. He thinks you're mysterious. He's created this whole enigma about you. The boy's completely smitten Lou, it's killing Zac. Anyway, we're going—*all of us*—are going to the movies in about...well, right now. There they are."

She's standing about twice as tall from this angle and growing every time I blink, her eyes set somewhere mid-way into the park. I don't look at them, I look at her, then Gustave jumps the short distance from the neighbours stairs to ours, weaves through her legs, then sits under our upstairs neighbours outdoor seat between our front doors where he pukes up some flowers. I point at it, but Selby overrules my input.

◇

"So, you can't talk huh?" DJ Simon asks.

I shake my head.

"Do you think the universe is trying to tell you something?" Zac asks.

This time I shrug.

"Is that why you left your bike discarded by Janice's fence like that?" Zac is at the head of the pack. I nod in response because I have no means of telling him that I had to fault the bike since there was no-one else around to blame. His response is to jump up and high-five some leaves hanging over the path. A few shake loose; those little helicopter leaves shaped like boomerangs. These ones aren't dry enough for spinning fluidity yet. Still pale green and full of juice.

"What if it's permanent?" DJ Simon asks, shadowing Zac. Our pace slows while the question lingers.

"It's not going to be permanent," Selby replies, clearly considering that a valid outcome. The subject changes and our pace increases. They speak of a TV show I haven't seen, a party I didn't go to and the potential for expansion in everyone. With nothing to offer, I drift to the back of the pack and tend to a rock in my flip-flop and dirt on my big toe.

In the middle of the otherwise clear sky, a plane leaves a white cloud of fuel. I thought it might be spelling me out a message that I'd need to survive the situation, but it wasn't. Unless there was something to the really big 'I' which eluded me.

Soon we're clipping ankles. The only redeeming quality of the congestion of foot traffic are the displays of imperfect golden splays of shine in varying angles and intensities reflecting off one building's windows onto neighbouring building's brickwork. I'm pointing out the phenomenon while we wait for the little green man to light up and permit us to continue, but I can't air the words to caption it. It seems like Zac and Selby are about to catch my gist but then the flow sweeps us away. DJ Simon's already halfway across the street and hasn't seen a thing.

As annoying and unwanted as the ambush—as any ambush, I imagine—a small percentage, say five percent, silently celebrates the prospect of sitting in a dark, climate-controlled room facing forward with established rules about talking. Unfortunately though, the rest of the world also shared this view, which turns our best seats in the house into the worst seats in the house. We're shoulder to shoulder and I can count only three exits for all these people.

At the base of the steps, two teenage couples stand stunned by the limited choices. I silently tell Selby I'm going to kill her and then tell her I wish she'd chosen some obscure foreign film so we might've had the cinema to ourselves. She doesn't respond.

"I'll be right back," Zac says, moving to the edge of his seat. "Gotta pee."

DJ Simon jumps up with nowhere to go. "I'll come. I need snacks. You guys want anything? Foods or beverages?"

Selby smiles '*no thanks*' and I shake my head, waiting for the screen to illuminate. I can feel her giving me a look for cracking my knuckles.

"No? No Maltesers, nothing? Ok, suit yourself."

Everyone in the aisle lifts their knees to make room for them. When they turn around to head down the corridor, Selby pushes her head into the seat-back for a panoramic view of the red velvet ceiling and exhales.

"I do love the cinema experience," she says. "But who's the ergonomic idiot who designed these chairs? Are they for people without spines?"

My right-side neighbour doesn't answer her and he doesn't look too agile either. She turns to me.

"So you really can't talk?"

I explain to her with a steely gaze that if I could talk, I would've put up an extraordinary debate that would've prevented this situation from occurring in the first place.

"What happened anyway? Did you ride into a wall or something?"

I mouth 'van' again and she gets up close to hear me, then leans back with closed eyes.

"I hate to be the one to tell you this, but I think you're just adding to the enigma."

I replicate her position but at about four hundred times more tense. Palms turned to the ceiling, ready to receive a miracle, but all I'm receiving are my neighbours heavy exhales. Must've been the same guy who sat next to Dynamite at the play.

Any exit.

Any exit.

Get out.

After the first sign of gunfire, I make my escape.

ATLAS

Atlas Chess Cafe goes back much further than one might assume on their first, second or third ride by, and it's home to the best wind tunnel in the city.

If the patron positions herself—or himself—horizontal on the couch facing the back exit, and the back door is open, it meets with this industrial sized fan about three feet wide, funnelling a cool and consistent breeze onto said patron. It's total bliss. The added benefit of it being a chess cafe only adds to the appeal. I know little of chess, I do know it's a game of silence and strategy and that bodes well for me.

Head toward the counter means it's cool on the legs.

Legs toward counter means it's cool on the face.

Today is a legs toward counter day.

This wind tunnel is in a pit section down three steps where four couches are arranged parallel to make two playing sections; each with a table between which have chess boards painted on top. No-one ever plays chess in the pit section. I think due to geriatric hips and accessibility concerns, so most of the action takes place at the front of the cafe, probably because it's the best light and most of the clientele have impaired vision. The minimal conversation and slow pace allows respite to come easy, as does the causal dress code typically involving knee length shorts, velcro sandals or tennis shoes with no laces and bright white socks that come half-way up clean tanned calves. It reminds me of a cruise ship where the only concern is maximizing the smorgasbord. Walking near any game will give off an aroma of cupboard lint and peppermints.

Opposite the pit is the raised section—same deal with accessibility. Limited use. It has fancier chess sets and overlooks the main counter where the lady—who's name I think is Lorraine—does the job of three, serving up cakes and coffees and teas and toasted sandwiches. She tolerates me well. I think she thinks I might bring in a younger demographic into the place. I'd never tell her it's not the case. She winks at me then flashes to a glance to the young man with a laptop on the couch shouldering mine, facing the front door. He's roughly my age with big silver headphones over his short brown hair. He's watching a movie which looks pirated and every now and then he puts some kind of hard candy in his mouth which breaks loudly. Lorriane doesn't seem to mind he's not interested in chess, nor that his feet are on the table with a coffee steaming between them. How he could drink a hot beverage on a day like today I did not know. I want to tell him to take his feet off the table, but I'm quickly drawn into the action on screen.

From what I can piece together, the main character is mad, a rogue spy or just mad and rogue. He doesn't say much—his lips haven't moved once since I tuned in. He appears to be trying to rescue this woman who is also silent and completely passive to many escape opportunities presented to her.

Trouble arises—for me, not for her—when she gets locked in a crate and the screen goes black so this guy's shiny headphones are in clear view and so am I and so is he; as if we were in the movie too, also with no lines. He's looking more amused than disturbed while I'm more stunned than anything else. Gun fire starts again and his face disappears and so does mine and blonde-guy-with-gun sideways dives from a flaming helicopter. Moments later, an open packet of Skittles appear in front of me.

We're close to the climax. I know this because the scenes flick quicker and the woman's got a gun to her head now. She's got blood streaking down her face but her hair is still commercial quality. Soon enough, the bad guy gets flattened and just as the troubled lovers are about to embrace, chatter in the chess cafe dims to near silence and the atmosphere stiffens. Over the laptop, two policemen make their way down the centre aisle while waiting eyes watch on, making silent bets about the identity of the trouble maker.

My co-viewer lifts his left headphone above his ear and I don't know if my best bet is to run out the back door or continue sinking into the depths of the couch. While I probably still had access to the $3.80 worth of damages, my bank balance would certainly be in deficit to fund the arbitrary amount of the fine due for smashing that croissant in Pascal's that day.

Lorraine is clutching a tea towel like she's got a secret of her own, but her angst eases when the cops beeline toward the raised section where one of the men goes '*ah fuck*' like he's just about to lose his Queen. There's just two silver-haired men in the fancy section, face to face with their elbows on the table, completely oblivious to the tension and the officers. The one in the red and blue hibiscus shirt leans back in his chair and crosses his arms over his chest, while the other one in the plain white button down gazes intensely at the chess board.

"Looks like I've finally one up-ed you Gary Baker," says Hibiscus Shirt.

The cops stand nearby, patiently waiting for attention to fall on them. Gary doesn't look too apprehensive about his fate, more disappointed he won't be able to finish the game. His indifference buys him a moment to move a piece.

"And that's check, mate."

Fifteen counts later, Gary's gone. The only evidence is his button still spinning on the floor from when it popped off his shirt during the hand-cuffing. After a few almost-moves and some head scratching querying the alternatives, Gary's opponent concedes defeat, re-sets the board, descends from his stool and meanders through the chess cafe, shuffling his feet as he takes stock of the other games on his way to the front door.

"Where ya going Bill?" someone asks from one of the side tables.

"I'm going for a swim," he says, not looking back. The credits roll and I too concede, a swim is the best idea I'd heard since...

ELEMENT

I have to concentrate otherwise I sink; my middle dips, my legs lower. The deeper I breathe the lighter I am, the better I float. Because of the quiet I can feel the tension overtly, mostly in my handlebar shoulders. It never ceases.

What's stuck there?

Again, I sink.

I'm lucky to get any air past my nasal cavity. Trying to coerce it is all that matters. The feedback is instantaneous. It's easier at this hour, without distractions, without whistles, without influence. It's easier in this element, without resistance, pressing up, pushing down.

I wonder what Gary did and my legs sink. Then I breathe in and my legs rise buoyant.

I wonder if Pascal knew it was me who slid the ten dollar bill under his door and I sink. I breathe in and my legs rise.

What if it's permanent? DJ Simon's words ring clear and I start to sink, but then a breeze carries over the surface and intake comes in warm and comforting. Night Jasmine, from Moongoggles. On that note I conclude that in light of recent events, it wouldn't be the worst thing.

Is it a lesson, like Zac suggested? To shut up more—that's what Dynamite said. I can't argue with his logic, in fact, right now I couldn't agree more.

Recycled words, day after day.

The same words, same stories, again and again.

HID.

HEAD.

HID.

HEAD.

I wonder if Rachel knows about the break-in and I sink, but this time I don't care to stay afloat. I relent, submerging, twisting, relishing as the sounds of the neighbourhood fall back so it's just... open, like my eyes, and the wider they get, the clearer it becomes. The sting is omnipresent, but I welcome it—the blur.

Light bounces off the tiled floor, continuous, random gleams and patterns. I'm probably wearing those patterns now—random, dancing, never stagnant. Disappearing and quickly replaced, disappearing and quickly replaced. I want to stay down here. This realm. This weightlessness. This element.

My body has other ideas.

Bubbles flee my nostrils, pockets of anxiety propelling me upwards. I breach the surface, eyes wide and furious with chlorine. Air floods my body, my veins, my head and chest, and in the darkness it all becomes very clear. I know exactly what I need to do.

REPROACH

Rachel's absent but the white mug is full and the PSOS folder is an arms length away. No footsteps down the corridor, just the ghost version of Dynamite swinging light in her chair asking me what good will it do anyway. The silence between seconds bears a message telling me to leave the letter on the desk and run.

Drop it and get out.

Go.

I'm convinced on *go*, then the door clicks open.

"Sorry I'm late Louise." Rachel knocks two books off her desk on the way to her chair. She analyses the mess, dismisses it and pulls herself in.

"So I bet—oh shit! What happened to your face?"

In lieu of answering, I offer her the letter. She looks between me and it before she takes it from me, scans the first page briefly and looks at me for answers. I divert my attention to the clouds moving behind the plant while she relaxes into her chair, covering her mouth with her right hand.

The first paragraph doesn't garner much more than a furrow. At one point she laughs an exhale from her nose. I imagine it's at the mention of the Elfman's hand on my back being the first thing I felt after impact. When she gets to the confession paragraph her legs switch their cross and my words project in the space between us.

..so if you felt an essence in your office last week, a foreign essence that didn't belong, your perception senses are in a better state of repair than mine. I infiltrated your workspace with another. The mission was mine – a quest to find the answers on a form I saw in here (your office) on the day we first met (the day of Sarah's absence).

The form belonged to a man I used to know. I kind-of knew him. I feel I know him now better now than I knew him then – does that makes sense? You see, he, Owen Fletcher, (do you remember him?) this Arabian princess and I were assigned to a study group to present a report on the alternate ways of diagnosing learning disorders, and as you may have gathered so far, the idea of group tasks chills me to my bones, and in my efforts to exempt myself from the horrible situation that it is speaking in front of an audience (of peers, no less) I suggested he alter his portion to suit me better, and to cut this story short, I haven't seen him since.

Please understand, my intention is not to sabotage your research project by being purposely difficult, it's all just a matter of circumstance and poor decisions unravelling at very inopportune times that coincide with the moments you are supposed to be receiving the data to advance your goals. Sometimes I just can't perceive the effect I have outside myself.

Also, I need to change a question on my form, if you still deem me eligible to continue.

Rachel tells me something over her glasses but I can't make it out. Her face is blank, exhibiting stellar professional conduct.

"So you rode into the back of a van and now you can't speak?"

I nod once.

"And you broke into my office?"

I nod again.

"And that's when you read these confidential files?"

I'm still at the bottom of the second nod, so I hold the position. She relaxes back in her chair and clasps her hands together.

"And yet, you sit here."

I tell her silently that I'm sorry and ask her how we'll go on from here. If I ran it wouldn't matter much, but I'm heavy in the chair.

"I've got a few theories Louise, but like you write—where was it..?" She scans the top half of page one. "Ah, here it is... *I noticed quickly how my responses were merely reactions.*"

The second-hand snaps electric currents through my handlebar shoulders. Right leg is manic. Left one is stone. She takes off her glasses. Eyes wide and glass.

"I'm about ready to react Louise, so perhaps you should come back next week and see what my response is on the matter."

A knock at the door punctuates her sentence and our meeting.

ARDENT

It takes most of the afternoon, three underpasses and some time in a vacant playground on a swing too small for my pelvis for that feeling—whatever it was—to fall away. I take to the backstreets and soon enough, I'm walking up that white stone path feeling more comfort in the idea of proximity than the prospect of home.

The courtyard holds this refreshing breeze, spinning in cycles from treetop to ground level, moving in a figure eight motion. It does well to cleanse me, cooling my hotspots and making inhales easier to come by. The sheets hanging out to dry give the wind a shape, an image of the power of it.

Since it's not Thursday, I sit in the proposal zone, flick off my shoes and try to coerce the breeze into my handlebar shoulders. It doesn't get much further than the space where I imagine my trachea to be.

Fortunately, the other residents of the Caledonian don't seem to care about my lingering. Only two enjoy the comfort of their balcony at this hour; one in blue shorts smoking and tending to his barbeque, and another in hair rollers and a night gown, hanging out her husband's jocks.

Some birds sing, others screech with insanity and the vibrations from apartment four come in bursts—waves of enthusiasm mostly from Aaron. A strange distortion alters their voices like they're sitting in a fishbowl.

"Alexis?"

"Hmm?"

"What's a doomsayer?"

Cutlery scrapes along a dinner plate.

"I think it's like it sounds: someone who goes around telling people they're going to die."

Moments later:

"That's a shitty job."

A woman who I suspect is 5DD carries two plastic bags bursting with groceries across the courtyard. Blue Shorts is alert to her arrival.

"Hey Alexis?"

"Hmm?"

"Do you find bizarre that we wake up every day as the same person?"

"Not really. Who else would we be?"

"I mean, if we're made up of atoms, how do we stick together and remain the same? Couldn't we morph into someone else overnight?"

"I suppose. I don't really know enough about it."

"Everyday I wake up and remember yesterday, so I'm reliving it. Today it's like, why has Jarrad turned against me? Oh right, he thinks I stole his sunglasses. And then it's like, how am I gonna spend that twenty bucks? Oh right, already spent it—those puzzles. Do you ever lay there before it all comes through?"

Alexis laughs. Cutlery hits the plate in finality. A chair scrapes along the floor.

"Sometimes man, but I have to wake up slowly for that to happen, which is rare. Usually it comes thick and fast and has this very demanding tone."

"I'm gonna wake up tomorrow and remember I won a million bucks."

I can't hear what Alexis' response is because a door slams so loud even Blue

Shorts hears it. He's looking right at me like he knows I don't belong in these parts. A staring contest is initiated, but he's a rookie and it doesn't take long before he backs down and turns his attention back to the barbeque. I take the opportunity to half-roll, half-crawl my way out of his sight, ending up on the grass behind a fern closer to their window. Their air-conditioner belts away at my feet.

A smaller door slams, probably the cereal cupboard door.

"What's up?" Aaron asks.

"There's no point talking about it." Dynamite responds.

"There's a point if it means you'll be making less noise." Alexis replies.

"There's no way to explain how fucked up it is. It's a deeply engrained disdain—inescapable and undescribable."

"How about go back to the beginning of the story so we know what you're on about."

Someone—Dynamite, I'm guessing—drops all their weight on the couch, surprising the air out of it.

"We had to give these kids this test today," He growls out irritation. "This Kognic test. And I'm handing them out feeling this... wrong-doing, deep in my marrow. I'm telling you man, it took every part of me not to let them go play and do them myself, if I knew the results wouldn't be stuck to them."

Silence from inside, two birds dart through the courtyard, weaving and dodging the leaves.

"Every day it's more and more clear to me. I mean, what if they're not here to learn these old things, this old stuff? What if they're here to make new stuff? Create completely new concepts?"

"They probably will then." Aaron offers.

"It's not even that though. What if it's not even that grandiose? What if even that is too much pressure? We bog them down by our old shit, pump it into them, then spend billions on think-tanks trying to figure out the problems, or ways to take advantage. The path is already innate within them, but we inundate them with our problems, and then try to fix it out of them."

"It happened to all of us Jarrad." Alexis says.

"You don't get it man, you've gotta see these kids — they're hyper-smart, not smart like intellectually, but yes, sometimes they are, but it's more like they're attuned, mad sensitive to every tiny nuance. They *know* man. And all these gradings and comparisons it's... I'm so tired of it."

The AC clicks gears. Blueshorts goes inside.

"So what do you propose we do?" Alexis asks sincerely.

"I don't know." Dynamite's answer is thick with despondency.

"Have you said any of this to your bosses?"

Dynamite laughs a laugh that's not really a laugh.

"No hope. Guy just talks at you, never to you. I went up to him the other day man. I tried to penetrate it, his ignorance. I said, *Look Robert, we've got shit to do here, so give me five minutes, hear what I've got to say, and then I'll hear you, then give me a second to process what you've just said and hopefully, we can work from there.*"

"And what'd he say?"

"He said he didn't have time, so I told him that's all he's got and then asked him what he's gonna do with it. He didn't like that."

ANTARCTICA

I'm about ten metres from the entrance to New Heights going too fast for
the turn. I continue straight, watching the ghost version of me curl off down the
footpath toward the glowing glass cube, wondering how much different my life is
going to be because I didn't take that turn. Wondering whether he's there tonight
and whether he can see more of the cosmos because of his goggles.

She—the ghost me—disappears out of view, replaced by a terracotta wall,
palm trunks and solar powered garden lights.

The hour brings perfectly isolated streets and silence helps with the underpasses. It also alludes me to the new music my bike makes post collision. Focus lies
on the repetative clicks of my busted gears which soothe me until I reach the city
stretch where shopfronts glow bright white and vacant from within and drunken
groups stagger onto the footpaths, encouraging extra push to my pedals.

This guy screaming at this girl outside a bar while this other girl is sitting on
the curb staring wide-eyed at the bitumen between her knees.

"No-one should talk to anyone like that," he yells at her, spit firing between
them "No-one ever."

She's looking glassy-eyed over his shoulders, not quite there. I don't blame her.

Cigarette for him. Cigarette for him.

Guy lying on the road.

Can't walk in those heels.

The angst propels me to Greenmere Park in no time, and that's when the flashes begin. Between me and the road the scenes blur, changing per streetlight.

That guy spitting. That man and the giant remote.

Tanzania spinning, landing on his knees.

Can't walk in those heels.

That look on Rachel's face.

The scenarios homogenize so I pedal even faster, trying to diffuse them. By Birchmore I'm white-knuckled, so tense I might pop. Pumping pedals. Knees lock. Quads burn.

A left turn would've taken me home in a minute, but again, the option goes on without me. Instead I go right down Birchmore, heading towards the canal. Velocity takes over, and tears run horizonal to my ears. Then this scream births out of me. I scream this animal scream originating from the pit of my heart, travelling raw along my vocal cords. The internal vibrations translate into this noise, this sound so removed, yet everywhere around me, and around this poor guy walking with reflectors on his backpack. Reflectors I see too late.

I'm rolling to the canal, no more effort required, no more effort to give. No stars are visable to superimpose on my tense spots. The sky's dark grey which amalgamates perfectly with my brain matter, providing zero clarity.

I'm wasted by the time I get to canal, barely able to step over the chain which is supposed to prevent people from entering the pier balcony after hours. It's useless security because most people can lift their knees, but I'm grateful the detail has been overlooked. I figure the person in charge of the pier balcony probably gets white-knuckled from time to time too. I pull myself up the stairs with what remains.

The drunk Swede is three seats down from his usual spot, about one inch tall from this angle. He's asleep with his head curved over to meet his knees. Behind him, the city glimmers. About forty percent of the lights are on. None close enough to make out any activity.

At the end of the balcony I lie on my stomach and look over the edge so I'm flying over the canal so quick I don't move. If I look behind me and to my right, city lights shimmer, and if I look straight down, the water is black gloss.

I'm flying, thinking, thinking I should stop milking this silence,

wondering why I'm happiest when I'm by myself,

hoping for a cool breeze to blow in from Antarctica.

SYZYGY

If their lights are off and the kitchen lights are off, and the hallway lights are off but the balcony lights are on and I'm sitting at the kitchen table looking toward the living room, the outside light shines through one of those ventilation bricks so five floating balls of light appear on the kitchen wall next to the laundry doors— still broken.

Warm air blows in every now and then, which feels like a message from Moongoggles. A receipt for my thoughts. I bet he's there right now, in that moon-chair. Of course he'd be there on the night I'm not. Our star gazing schedules have misaligned, so tonight it's the five floating balls instead.

I don't have my own snorkel gear and without it, immersion is limited and less encompassing. Timed, not timeless. And breathing apparatus aside, I don't feel quite as safe without him there, laying guard, with that peaceful look on his face.

Part Three

RECALIBRATION

INSOUCIANCE

"Don't worry, we're cool." Amina senses my concern as I look around the auditorium, feeling unease. It's a strange sensation, like I've entered a scene of a movie half-watched in my youth, the kind that curls the stomach and should be turned off but the remote isn't anywhere.

She enters a vacant row and sits on the third seat in behind three girls already situated. I take the second seat in watching as she positions her textbook at her lower back, making assorted faces of torture until she finds the sweet spot.

"Are you sure about this?" My question comes out in a voice unfamiliar and much louder than I intend. "Seems like a small class."

"We're early. They'll pile in soon and you'll be rendered invisible, trust me."

I shift down in my seat to make the most of the human shields. People enter from both sides of the auditorium, some in groups, some individually. Amina's flicking her pen against the front of a three-ringed binder.

"Who would you say your dream guy is?" She asks this while watching her peers filter in the right entrance. I consider her question carefully in the blue-grey seatbacks.

"I think I'd say... Rocky—the original."

"Okay, so close your eyes and imagine Rocky the Original walks in the east entrance and sits in the seat in front of you. What do you do?"

"I leave him there."

She gives me a deadened look. "No, really. Give it more than your knee-jerk response, please."

I close my eyes and try to concentrate. It takes a while, but eventually the neon shapes form into a young Stallone. He's dressed in grey sweats and holding a basketball which he bounces three times as he crosses the room and once on the stairs we just walked up. He falls into the seat in front of me, left arm stretched out along the backrest and the b-ball spinning on his right index finger.

"I was right," I tell her. "I leave him there."

When I open my eyes the exact opposite of a young Stallone appears. Well, maybe not the exact opposite, but Zac, which isn't close at all. Things get worse when Rachel appears behind him and heads straight for the lectern. When she gets there she puts her laptop bag down and positions herself behind the stand grabbing the edges as if *she's* the one who needs to hold on.

Vibrations dull to silence. I slide down further in my seat so I can't see her therefore she can't see me.

"Are you ok?" Amina whispers.

"I'll have to tell you later."

"Very few people show much of themselves," Rachel's voice fills the room without need for a microphone. "People have their reasons—a whole lifetime worth of reasons. What is seen is unlikely to be the true self. We hide for a myriad of reasons—all perfectly justified of course, so if you want to learn a person, you must learn to look at the space between. You'll find out a lot in what people say, and moreover, you'll find a world of answers in the absence of words."

Rachel walks. I count four steps. Based on Amina's head position, she's at stage-right, in line with Zac. I peek between heads and Rachel spots me instantly.

"Wide scope, huh?" Everyone finds that funny except me. "There're two streams of thought here. First, there's listening versus hearing. You can listen, but where's your concentration? Are you listening to the words and missing the subtext? Are you barely there and picking out keywords only? What about their pitch? Are you listening for pauses? For silence? Are there rhythms to their speech? Where are the long answers and where are the short ones? Are you hearing what you want to hear? Are you asking certain things, hoping for certain answers? Are you hearing what they want you to hear?"

I drop my head closer to my knees both to stay hidden and for circulation purposes. Amina remains perturbed, teetering on amused until her smile disappears like maybe we're not as invisible as she might've hoped.

"You can listen with all your senses. You can listen to the colour of voice, to the expression behind the words, to the mix of the atmosphere in which the discussion takes place. Listen for shortness of breath, solemn sighs, peaks of excitement, sudden withdrawals of comment. If you tune into these variables you will receive an intensified report. It becomes richer. You're listening."

"Then why don't we?"

I don't have to look up to know who asks the question. It sure isn't Rocky the Original.

"Fear."

The word comes out in the shape of a sphere; a glass ball that grows to encompass and silence the whole space. According to Amina's gaze, Rachel's on her way back to the podium.

"Fear you will hear something you don't want to hear. Fear what you know won't be true anymore. Fear you'll see a mirror of your faults and fear your truth will lose its footing. Those kinds of realisations can really shake your world down. It takes a lot to let a person in, and you don't have to be the one talking for that to happen."

Everyone's listening, that's for sure. No sounds of pen on paper. No rustling of notes. No fingers on keys. Zac not insisting on the last word makes for a notable silence.

"Everything is perspective, and there are lessons to be learned from silence, from listening. We don't listen anymore. To others, to ourselves. What is it we're saying? These stories? What is it we're seeing? What's our focus. Because the frames we choose—we can choose other ones. Everyone gets to choose. Of course it feels weird at first, but all new shoes do."

A few people laugh while I dust mud off my laces.

"Did you recently switch into this class?"

The question lingers over my seat but Amina's looking in Zac's direction. Her whole body stiffens, captivated.

"I did," Zac says. Rachel walks two steps. "Don't check the enrolment though."

A few muffled sniggers shake the tension loose, but the anticipation is too much for Zac. His chair bottom hits the seatback and I can imagine exactly what he looks like bolting out of the room with his backpack hugged to his chest.

"Could the other people not paying tuition fees please be also standing?"

It really isn't as bad as I expected, mostly because of this numbing disjoint that already has me outside, walking down the front steps toward the torrent of foot traffic, sun shining down on me. The worst part is seeing Amina melt into her seat.

"I'm sorry," I tell her on a breath. "I'll wait outside. I have a riddle for you."

⟡

People come and go in waves, herded by cars, winding around the man on the floor with a cardboard box splayed out beneath him. It creates a safe perimetre around him which no-one goes near, except two little kids who become enthralled by the contents of his trolley for a brief moment until their mothers—I assume—call them back to the table. That's about when this figure blocks out the sun and I look up to see Hazif standing there, banana in one hand, backpack strap in the other.

"You look worried," He slumps down next to me so the bench is at full capacity.

"I am worried."

"Anything I can help with? I've been putting out fires all over the place today." He takes a bite of his banana and the smell travels over.

"I wouldn't know where to begin. I'm waiting for Amina. She's in class over there." I point across the street, noticing for the first time the tired on his face.

"How many lunches did you make today?"

"None. No more lunches. No more cooking."

"No longer symbiotic?"

Some banana goes down the wrong pipe.

"That's right," he coughs, looking sideways to the billboard I'm trying to avoid. "Hey, I gotta head. Tell 'Mina I said hey. Ask her to call me."

When the clock strikes twenty-seven degrees, Amina appears. She stops on the top step to put her books in her bag.

"Did she say anything?" I ask her.

"I didn't stick around to find out. You want to walk with me to my next class? It's on LaTrobe. You can tell me your riddle on the way."

Because of her pace and the manic surroundings, the recount of my failed mission comes out in a hurried mess. I feel sure I've glossed over the important details and spent too much time emphasising key flaws in my deductive reasoning.

"So what'd it say?"

"It wasn't there."

"Are you sure?"

"Yeah I'm sure. I mean, I'm as sure as a person can be who saw it for about three seconds initially, which was enough to make a notable and significant emotional response to it, which led to a scheme to claim its possession only to later find it either a) didn't exist, or b) had been removed."

"That sure, huh?"

"It's going to be extra awkward going back there now. "

The little red man indicates we better stop walking which gives Amina the opportunity to check my face, once again, for signs of head trauma.

"You're going to go back? Even though she just caught you auditing her class and you broke into her office?"

"And confessed to it, did I mention that?"

"No, you didn't."

The man changes to green and we walk. "I don't get it—how's it there, then it's not?"

She doesn't answer me because my question is unanswerable. We're halfway down LaTrobe when she speaks again.

"Do you mind if we sit down for a minute?"

"Not at all."

Some concrete squares outside a printing shop next to some pigeons provide the seating for the respite. A languid fellow is watching the birds. He's wearing a scarf despite the warm weather.

Amina twists to her right and tension pops from within. She seems satisfied with the release.

"After your departure—which you took rather gracefully, I must say, not sure about the bow though, but anyway—Rachel said this thing, and I'm probably going to mess up the phrasing, but you know how she was talking about the mix of the atmosphere and hearing what you want to hear?"

"Yeah."

"Well, she said because our brains need to organise all this data coming at us, decipher it and organise it, we tend to ignore the sensations that arise once certain stimuli is introduced—muscle tension, shortness of breath, etcetera."

"Like my handlebar shoulders."

Her expression is a question. "I'm guessing it's like it sounds?"

"Yes."

"Right. Sure, like your handlebar shoulders. So they're like indicators, these sensations, always happening, all day long, all the time, but because we're busy compartmentalising everything, turning people, feelings, situations into this mental idea, and because the data is coming in so. damn. fast, those sensations get over-ruled for these generic concrete labels based on past experiences. So we're missing out on this whole other aspect." Her hands fall into her lap and her brows furrow. "I'm not explaining this right, am I?"

"I'm following."

"She said it much better."

Amina shifts to face west instead of north so her back is toward me. She points to a spot near her spine, just below her ribcage.

"Do you think you could press your index and middle finger knuckle really hard right here and hold it there?"

She clasps her fingers behind her head so her elbows are wide. I do as I'm asked while the languid fellow watches. I try not to notice his attention as I feel Amina's own version of my handlebar shoulders. It's a pebble, about two inches, solid and stuck near her spine. I press into it with my knuckles like she asked, plac-ing my palm on the other side of her spine. She turns her head left to right.

"So I was thinking how useless is it attributing that word to Amal. By associ-ating the word it's perpetuating this focal point, solidifying the potentiality of what could be—*what is*—a flux state."

"I guess that's the starting point to treatment though."

Her fingers unclasp and her arms fall to her side and I feel the weight of her deflation as she looks over her right shoulder with this intensity that makes me feel like I've said the wrong thing.

"But we miss out on so much."

It goes left eye, right eye, left eye, right and then for the briefest moment, my shoulders disengage, enabling an exchange; these waves of blame, shame and guilt cross between us about all the things we talk about and alot of the things we don't. A catharsis of sorts, unspoken but registered none-the-less. A car horn sounds and the street re-emerges after having momentarily dissolved completely.

"What are we going to do about it?" I ask her softly.

"I don't know yet."

She adjusts her position on the concrete square so we're both facing the same direction, short of feeling good about it, even though we want to.

"I think I do too much," she says.

"Maybe too much of what you don't like."

"Yeah, probably."

"Do you see anyone about it?" I ask. "Your back, I mean."

She wriggles from her hips, little movements left to right and back again.

"I see the physio once a week, but it's been a lot better since I started stretch-ing. I stretch in the park for an hour every morning before I do anything else. With the shopkeeper from the deli, believe it or not. I'm pretty sure he knows I'm there." She squints into the sun, the smallest smile emerges as she absorbs the warm rays. "You know what? Screw Ethics. I couldn't sit in that chair for ninety minutes. It'd kill me."

"You're gonna skip it?"

"Everything in my body is saying so. There's no point in going anyway, the professor is this super weird guy, I can barely understand him. He uses visual aids which have no relationship with the content of his talk. It's like he's trying to get his point across subliminally but I need it to be bliminal at one o'clock on a Friday afternoon."

She slides off the concrete square and puts her bag on her back.

"I'm going for a swim. You wanna come?"

"I wish I could," I tell her. "But I've got a meeting."

C-SECTION

My inner compass guides me to the C-section but stops working after that. Fortunately, not a lot of people have elbow-length blonde dreads in the department so it doesn't take long before someone directs me to C-11. Before I know it I'm semi-reclined and lubricant is cooling my scalp.

Dread's is pretty methodicas she applies the electrodes, and in the way she talks about her boyfriend, which is the main topic of our one-way conversation. After about every third criticism, she pauses, takes a breath and counters her point.

"He's just lazy. He thinks if he bides his time inspirations gonna come rolling through on a Jeep Cherokee. Doesn't shower much either." Inhales. "I can't see myself with anyone else though."

I make an agreeable sound. It's all I wish to offer on the matter.

"So what kind of music will I be listening to?"

My question echoes three times at full length while she sorts through the electrodes.

"The music? A few different kinds; classical and contemporary, some you'll recognize, some you might not. What happened to your neck here?"

"Oh, I crashed into the back of a stationary vehicle."

"How did that happen?"

"I wasn't looking where I was going. Couldn't speak for a week."

"Really?"

"Yeah, I didn't know that could happen either. Truth be told, when I woke up and remembered I didn't have to say anything, my whole body relaxed. It's so liberating not having to deal with the fallout from your own word selection. Do you ever get that?"

She attaches another suction cup, pressing down firmly and wiping off the excess lube.

"No, never."

Dreads is fiddling with some wires when this buzzer sounds, startling both of us. She grabs a towel and wipes her hands, then picks up the phone on the wall by the door with two fingers.

"Rayna." Her eyebrows raise. "Oh right. No problem. I'll be right there."

She hangs up and looks between my head and the clock.

"I have to go unlock a door. Be back in a minute."

And she's gone. Her footsteps have a different ring to themcompared to Rachel's. I transcribe them saying: *three hours in a dark room for a hundred bucks? Nut—not worth it*. Even though the likelihood I'd see her in the hall while escaping didn't fall in my favour, my choices felt limited, so I disconnect and take flight.

−◈−

Halfway down the corridor the extent of my over-reaction flashes obnoxious. Waves of fluroescent light pulse, infusing my skin with this drab tone that goes: *rent. bills. rent. rent. bills*. Someone's calling my name, so I jump the last few stairs which brings about a wave of vertigo and those flying white dots again, telling me I've gone completely off the rails.

The quad is bright, saturated, covered in a blue hue. Silhouettes cut through; more than someone with a slicked head could hope for. Buildings, trees and fences bend into form, as does the bike rack, and my bike is not in it.

"Are you in the middle of something?"

Rachel's behind me. The ground spins the opposite direction beneath me. She's searching for something in her bag.

"Not anymore," I tell her.

"I have to apologise for my lack of professionalism the other day." She holds out an envelope between us. "Here's the first half of your compensation. I forgot to pass it on to Tanya when I asked her to cover for me. If you can still make it for the last session and the interview, I'd appreciate it. Is our usual time in a week okay?"

It's like nothing off-kilter has transpired at all. Her expression is calm, expectant. Eventually I manage a nod and take the envelope from her. Beyond the glare of her glasses she looks appreciative, then she goes inside without saying a word about the break-in, the auditing or my hair.

NORMA MERMAID

Wiped clean of all dignity, I'm on the home stretch and matters feel like they might start levelling out to bearable, but then I notice yellow crime scene tape zig-zagging up the front stairs of our walk-up and all hope is lost. I make the mistake of looking toward the school for answers only to find Mrs Egg Salad Sandwich pointing an accusatory finger in my direction, mouthing something to this silver-haired woman next to her decked out in work-out clothes. She's advancing toward me at a considered pace, her intentions becoming clearer with every step — she's planning an intersept. Obviously I couldn't go upstairs and let them know where I live, so I run.

Four blocks from home and three from the pool, the voice of God falls over me.

"Young lady, what are you running from?"

The voice of God belongs to Neil. Out of the water and fully clothed, Neil is much larger than he appears when he's just a floating head. He's standing two steps up in the doorway of the barbers — half-in, half-out.

"Well, Neil... I'm fleeing from an old lady... a concerned parent, grandparent — and, or — concerned teacher."

"Looks like you could use a chair." Neil's head goes more in the barbers than out. "We'll just have to get rid'a this old melon."

The 'old melon' Neil is referring to makes himself known by waving beyond the gloss of the street reflecting in the shop window. He's sitting on a stool, framed by sun-faded posters of outdated hairstyles not cool since Melrose Place. One gold tooth is smiling at me, then the stool pops up and he's in the doorway, rubbing his ancient jaw.

"Better sharpen that razor, old man," he tells Neil. "Keep your equipment up to industry standard, because you, my friend, aren't."

"Tell it to the committee, prune."

Goldtooth's out the door and he needs the handrail so I retreat a few steps. A quick scan of the vicinity confirms no seasoned athletes are on my tail. Goldtooth smells musky. He's well tanned, skeletal and winks at me as he passes, and although he's not wearing a hat, he dips his head like he is, then flicks a wave to Neil.

"See you at dawn, peppercorn."

Neil stands aside to let me in.

The barbers could hold about eight Neil's if he were multiplied. Despite the small square footage, cool tiles and wall length mirrors keep the place airy and the four hanging baskets of plants show that organisms could survive and flourish. The walls are yellow and leak streaked, but not in a dank way, more dated, and there's a shelf on the wall opposite the mirrors, hosting upwards of twenty palm-sized photo frames.

Neil sits on a stool behind the cutting chair which looks like it's been around since the turn of the century. He's looking out the window while two fast moving women walk by on the other side of the street, and I'm relieved to find it's not a retrieval mission, just a pair keeping fit, sporting matching pink and lavender visors. Neil waves.

"Hello girls, how you keeping? Alright?"

They both wave back and are out of view in the same breath. Neil analyses the back of my head, his steel wool eyebrows dancing confusion.

"Rough day?"

"It's been a surprise to say the least," I tell him. "It's not usually this greasy. An unfortunate situation came about earlier today where I had an allergic reaction mid-experiment and I had to leave before they could wash the lube out of my hair."

Neil starts pulling up wet chunks of hair like we're old friends and none of this is very unusual.

"When was the last time you got a haircut?" he asks.

I shrug and he pulls his stool in.

"I really don't know how to answer that one Neil."

"It's a good job you came in when you did."

"Why's that?"

"Well, it's five to four now and I shut at six—we might just make it." His smile lines indent and his reflection winks at me. "We better get this head in the sink."

Two strides later, cool water is streaming over my head, down my neck and into my ears. It's bliss.

"The melon seems like a pleasant fellow."

"Marty? He'll keep," Neil's pumping shampoo. "Still dives like a pin drop, I'll give him that. Same as he was fifty years ago."

"Over at Birchmore?"

Neil nods. "Every day for fifty years."

"I've never seen his gold tooth before. I do have tunnel vision though."

"Still dives like a pin, but he's got a whole bank of problems, that Marty."

"A whole bank?"

Neil turns off the tap with his elbow and starts lathering on shampoo. My head feels tiny in his seasoned hands. I press outward into them hoping he might have the magic touch that'd activate my amygdala.

"Well for one, he'll *yeah, but* his way around everything. Anything I say it's always, *yeah, but*. The other day I'm trimming his mo' and I ask him, I said, *Marty, have you tried that granola breakfast cereal? It's really good*. He goes, *yeah, but, it gets stuck in me teeth, all those bits*. Then, when I'm trimming his eyebrows, I tell him, *Marty, you gotta look after yourself, no more whiskey for breakfast*. He goes, *yeah, but, I'm gonna die anyway, probably real soon with all these terrorists*." Neil shakes his head. "And today I said, *Marty, sometimes I think Norma's here, moving around and telling me things*. He goes, *yeah, but, she's dead*. Like I said, the man banks his problems."

Though I can't tell exactly because there's a significant amount of shampoo in my eyes, but it looks as though Neil's lost in a photo.

"Norma's my wife."

He leans over me to grab a small oval frame. It smells like he's got peppermints in his shirt pocket. He holds out this small gold oval frame housing a black and white picture of an elegant woman sitting on the edge of a bed; classic roller curls, dark lips, high penciled eyebrows.

"My face is weathered beyond but my heart is young because it's still in love." He muses the sentence then replaces the photo on the shelf and tilts it just so, then turns the tap on again and starts wringing out my hair.

"Pardon my old man sentiments love, I get nostalgic. It happens when you're old."

"You're not old," I tell him.

"I'm twenty-one times three plus two."

"An old man wouldn't have the faculties to do math like that."

He bellows a laugh. "You're kind. I'm just well rehearsed. See here's proof.." And he dips his head to show me some bald gloss starting to emerge at the top of his head to demonstrate his point. The rest of his head is covered in silver strands.

"Age is ambiguous anyway."

"Is it?"

"I think so."

He throws a towel over my face, cutting off my tunnel vision completely, then makes his way back to the cutting chair which is cue for me to get up and join him. No conditioner.

When I get there, I notice the picture of Norma is perfectly positioned so he can see her in the reflection as he cuts. It's no wonder he doesn't mind the limited confines—he's only partially there. The rest of him is in a parallel dimension with Norma. He picks up a comb and tends to my split ends.

"Three winters ago, for forty-one days, not one customer came in, not even Marty who's normally round here like a fly on Christmas dinner. Every Tuesday and Friday for nineteen years he comes in for a mo trim, and not even he ventured through that storm. Do you remember it?"

"Yeah, I remember." The comb is stuck so he switches for another one with a wider tooth.

"Not one person, except my Norma. I don't give one hoot about what that old onion thinks, she comes by here alright. She comes in on a breeze, on a gust. I think I learnt as much about her in those forty-one days as I did in forty-seven years of marriage."

He takes a respite, looking out the window, resting his hands in his lap. A car sweeps by and he returns, looking to my reflection then picking out a section of hair, holding it horizontal. He's smiling the same smile as that day watching the lady in the community garden tossing dirt over her shoulder.

"What'd you learn?" I ask him, as he works on a tangled clump,

"What did I learn? Oh, I learnt it all. I still learn, all too late of course, but that's life sometimes." He's having no luck with the knot so he leaves it and starts on another section. "I learnt how important it is not to pull everything you need from one person—hearts get weak that way. I learnt how patient she was, how she was the perfect amount of selfish and selfless. She said I was the scum of the earth and that I made her crazy and she liked it that way. She said it kept her sane." He smiles widely at me. "What? What's so funny? You don't believe me, do you? You think I'm a decrepit old nut job?"

"No, it's... you said you made her crazy, did she say that or is that what you think?"

"She told me. Why?"

"Seems like that's the part we're all trying to fix."

"Oh no. No, don't do that."

The visor women come by again. Neil waves once more, then rolls around my left shoulder to reach for a spray bottle. He starts squirting the knots. It smells of flowers and salt water.

"What's it like when she visits?"

Either the smell or the memory envokes a dreamy look on his face. Probably the memory. His forehead softens, hairline retreats half an inch.

"It's like when you listen to one of those good, good old songs, but imagine you're a stiff, rigid old man—like Marty—all crippled, skin and bone, and then this breeze comes in. She blows on in like a wave, filling in every crevice of the rock face. That's what it's like. People don't believe it. Marty laughs and calls me a crazy old bat, but I feel it, and I'll tell you this love—you can't argue experience. I should know, I have a lot of it."

He smiles widely at me. Teeth stained like the walls.

"I remember in our first year of marriage, I'd get so mad at her for leaving little droplets of water in the shower—can you believe that? It's a shower for Pete's sake." He shakes his head, puts the bottle down and rolls around me.

"Sometimes you just gotta laugh at how foolish you were when you thought you knew everything, you know?"

"I do know Neil."

He combs through the abandoned section with ease, then adjusts my head so my chin is nearer my chest and starts dividing my hair into sections.

"You hold your breath and don't make use of the exhale."

Through the slicks of hair I silently prompt his reflection to go on.

"When you go under—you hold it in and then panic and it's all gone in an instant, so the next inhale is minimal. You gotta let the bubbles out slow. If you let them out slow and fill them with what you don't need, when you come up, it'll be like the wave and the rock face. It'll fill you right up, more and more every time, but you gotta pay attention. Just try, you'll notice the difference, you'll be able to stay under longer, mark my word. Did you see the one about the Beluga Mermaid? In Russia, I think. Stark naked she does it. Holds her breath for nine minutes."

"Eleven," I correct him.

"Was it eleven, was it?" He holds the comb up to his collarbone. "I'm up here most of the time, but I'm getting better. Norma's always told me to slow down. She said I did everything too fast. *You think too fast, you move too fast.* So I swim. It tempers me, forces me to notice, in the pool and out of it. If you just relax and trust there's air for you when you resurface, everything will feel much easier."

"Yeah, but... " my rebuttle earns me a hair pulling. "I don't know how to relax."

He shakes his head.

"That's the problem with you lot. You trouble yourselves expecting immediate results then get angry when the postman doesn't come."

"Well, how do you relax?"

"I dream of Norma."

"I don't think that'll help me."

"Are you in love?"

"No."

"Ah... you'll know it when you see it."

"I don't think it works like that anymore."

"No?"

I shake my head.

"That's another problem with us lot, we've got too much to choose from and have been forced to define ourselves so strongly that we've got little tolerance for understanding others to the point of unconditional love."

Neil frowns at my split ends, floats a light nod, then looks at Norma.

"That's a shame," he says. "Are you speaking simply for yourself though?"

He tugs a section of hair again to ensure the echo of his question penetrates my hair follicles.

Am I speaking simply for myself?

Probably.

Of course.

"Just notice," he implores. "Train all day. It will help with everything. For me, I moved too fast so I started swimming. I had so much left to say, so I started talking to her. You just gotta figure out a way to channel it."

I notice alright. I notice my nose-hairs are woven together and I'm hardly getting a tablespoons.

The two ladies walk by again on the other side of the street. Elbows at right angles, gone in three strides. Neil picks up his scissors.

"All over the news that beluga mermaid."

"I wish it wasn't to keep them captive though."

Barely a teaspoon.

"Maybe it isn't. You can never know these things for sure."

BUSTED

I'm waist deep with no-where to hide and even before he appeared, I sensed him. Now we're stuck in the moment of fright before flight, both inanimate, waiting for the other to move first.

Two cars go by and we tell each other what's going to happen next and it's news I do not like. He moves first, rapidly for a man of his circumfrence. His white shirt traces the fence, then he's out of sight momentarily, disappearing behind the change-room building.

"Hey you!" his voice is guttural, desperate, excited, and perhaps a little scared. "Hey you! Stay right there."

Resistance presses heavy from all angles like I'm not moving at all. Litres fall off me as I climb the ladder, more than I thought would be possible. I jump over the blue man hole cover, run passed the sun-chairs and start clawi my way up the fence. Inner thigh scrapes on wire as I climb over. Dirt sponges between my toes as I land.

I've got about fifty metres on him and a community garden to navigate.

Sticks stab, nothing is defined.

Teeth knock. Concrete jars.

Another fence.

Streetlight after streetlight.

Everything reflects.

If I run fast enough maybe I'll turn into dots and he'll tackle me and there'll be nothing to grab because I'm dots.

I feel like a singular, solid, dense dot not getting far at all.

If any birds were watching, they'd note a drastic reduction in my pace.

Behind me: glowing and bouncing. Streetlights.

Next to me: tree trunk, rubbish bin, bus stop. Vomit.

Up ahead: houses, fences, hedge about hip high.

I launch.

One leg hits the ground, then the other. Grass is wet. Cold. Recently watered.

Stillness.

No footsteps.

No breath.

Not mine. Not his.

TV glows inside the house. Rose bushes line the path to the front door. Leaves rustle above like nothing odd is happening. I lay braced, waiting.

Handlebar ribcage.

Nothing in, nothing out.

A line of cloud divides the night sky. It's about an inch thick from this angle, glowing grey and travelling slowly toward the moon

Silence.

I imagine if I stay still long enough, when the cloud travels over me, it'll cleanse me, scanning over my body and wiping out my black spots.

A door clicks open.

"Hey you! GET THE FUCK OFF MY GRASS!"

Of everything I thought might happen today, none of it did.

PRECIPICE

The crime scene tape is merely caution tape that someone's broken and tied to the railing to enable access. Turns out I didn't blow the place up, but when I discover we're hosting a party in some ways I wish I did.

I'm about to attempt a swift entry through my bedroom window when a couple begins their ascent behind me, forcing me to use the front door. My reward for conforming to normal social conduct is a panel of disapproving looks from three girls standing in the hallway looking me up and down like my name's Mary.

Through the judgmental deluge, Selby appears, and her party spirit folds out of her as she scans the length of me. It slides off somewhere under Zac's desk.

"This is weird because your hair looks... better than I've ever seen it, but the rest of you is literally covered in filth."

She's absolutely right so there's not much to say on the matter. The couple enters behind me so I'm pinned to one side of the hallway, Selby at the other. The three girls weave through us, and the couple, heading for the front door which I lock behind them. Selby gives me a look, then unlocks it and checks to see if they noticed, while I close my eyes, hoping this reality is but a room of shapes and delusion escapable if I open my eyes.

"What happened to you?" She dusts something off my leg.

"I went for a bathe."

"Up a riverbank? Why are you so dirty?"

"Sel, why are all these people in our house when someone's clearly deemed it unsafe?"

"Oh, you mean the tape? That's just precautionary."

"No, it's actual caution tape, which means we're passed the point of *pre*-caution."

She nods in agreement. "You make a good point, but it's the play's finale tonight and it was already planned. It was too late to change it. Don't worry about it though, I'll make a sign directing everyone up the fire escape. No problem."

"What's with the tape?"

"You'll have to ask Zac. Now, come with me." She grabs my wrist and leads me down the hall.

Our kitchen is full of people—the worst condition it could be in. Some guy's using my mug, the laundry doors remain horizontal on the floor more broken thanks to Allan's interference. Selby knocks four times on the bathroom door and the pipes bang to life indicating whoever is in there is winding things up. She's standing foot from my face with her arms crossed telling me she's concerned, confused and maybe fed up. I shake my head.

"Allan's useless, isn't he?"

"What's going on?"

"You mean my outfit?" I look down at my mud-crusted clothes. "I really can't explain it. Sometimes I feel like my clothes are wearing me."

"You know what I mean."

"There's nothing to discuss, really. A minor civil misunderstanding."

"Oh yeah?"

She's not reassured and takes it out on the door.

"Lloyd's coming tonight."

I'm assessing her seriousness when the door swings open presenting an up-close Cornelius. He and Selby trade places—him out and her in. She pulls me in behind her, closing the door while I kick the toilet seat down to assess my injuries. Selby hands me a wringed-out facecloth, then starts smoothing out her face in the mirror.

"DJ Simon too. He's all about you Lou. He thinks you're an enigma."

No. No. No.

"I'm not sure of a lot of things, Sel, but I'm absolutely, completely certain when I tell you there are no avenues for romance in my life right now. I'm barely breathing when I'm by myself, surrounded by trees, in wide open spaces."

Her reflection sighs.

"I'm not suggesting you marry him."

I sigh too.

I know.

"How's Zac?"

Her shoulders fall on receipt of my question followed by a momentary pause from tending to her curls. Then her back straightens and her chin lifts slightly.

"I'm trying to centre myself first," she tells her reflection. "I'm too co-dependent for my ideal of independence. First me, then us, otherwise my efforts are futile."

She looks mad, then puzzled, then secures a section of hair with a bobby pin and looks at me, then to the tiles.

"It makes sense in my head. Like maybe I'm striving for something that isn't really what I want, but what I feel like I'm supposed to want. I get mad at him because he doesn't get it, but I'm not even clear of what I want him to get. I think that's the issue. How can I expect him to understand if I can't explain it right?"

"Do you think you expect him to understand?"

"Yeah, I do."

I wipe over my muddy shin to reveal a congealed blood pattern like some-one's got me with a swift swipe of sandpaper. The graze on my inner thigh is a quarter the size I imagined it would be. Raised edges and bright red in the centre.

"I do feel like I'm getting better though. He's so patient with me." Selby turns back to the mirror and takes out the bobby-pin. "Did you hear me about Lloyd?"

"Yes. And I heard you about Simon too."

Four flannel rinses later and congestion has intensified ten-fold. To equate it to a circus would be insulting to the art form. Voices meddle, mosquito repellant inundates and negatives overlay faces with every heavy blink.

Just notice.

Train all day.

I notice alright. I notice one blocked nostril and I notice strangers pouring their bodies over my furniture. My bedroom—thankfully vacant—offers marginal relief, but then I also notice the contents of my wardrobe is either in my laundry basket or look like pyjamas. The situation is hopeless. Being horizontal helps with oxygen intake, and I'm gifted with a breeze, steady and warm.

You gotta let it out slow.

I'm almost getting a full tablespoon when the front steps creak. A man's voice travels up before he does. Unless it's Allan, my position flush against the wall should keep me hidden. A lot of questions are being aired, all of which go unan-swered.

"Shit, when?"

"How long?"

"Should I tell them?"

It's not Allan, it's Harris. His foreign curls repeat in my mirror, phone at his ear and eyes on the next step. At the front door he pauses out of sight but less than a metre away. Too much party static prevents me from hearing the next thing he says. Covertly, I switch to the opposite end of the bed for a better vantage point.

It's like one step forward, eight steps back; Harris enters, three people leave and those girls come back having multiplied. They don't have any qualms about peering in my window. One girl gets forehead deep and the fright of her life.

In my darkened room the hope of two things illuminate which might just salvage this situation:

1. Harris decides to abandon the festivities and invites me along to meet up with Alexis and Co. at the falafel shop—sans Triptochen.

2. Following a quick hello and a few laps of surveillance, I discover the pool security guard has retired for the evening believing the adage that criminals never return to the scene of the crime.

People move a helpful centimetre but not much more. Matters get worse when I enter the living room and notice Blonde Dreads standing by the kitchen door looking stunned to see me. She's connected to he-who-must-be-her-boyfriend.

"No shit!" is her response after a moment placing me.

It's such a disbelieving tone that the immediate vicinity quietens to inspect the subject—*me*—and for some reason I don't move much, or say anything. Someone coughs to exacerbate the awkwardness and the music drops to a different frequency.

"That's the one who escaped mid-experiment."

I know she didn't *mean* to announce it so accusatorily. More like she's narrating her mental connections as they occur. Although it's not pleasant, it's really not that bad. I'm standing there interested in what happens next.

When you're composed, they don't know what to do.

That's when a hand presses down on my shoulder, heavy and firm, as if the party gods have arrived to penalize me for my antisocial spirit.

Is it the security guard?

Allan?

No. None of the above.

I turn and I'm faced with a dark grey torso about four times the width of me.

"You're a hard woman to track down." Lloyd's studying my face and looks confounded by his findings. "Jesus Lou, you look like I could use a drink."

Between us, a freshly popped beer bottle appears. It's connected to Cornelius who's happy to provide the service.

"Here ya go, buddy. Great season man."

Gracious as ever, Lloyd accepts the beer and clinks bottlenecks with Cornelius. In this light he looks browner, certainly older, either like he's matured or like he's been tackled head-high too many times. Whatever it is, the marks of wear work for him.

Now Dreads is silent, and her lover and the rest of the living room remain paused for the next move.

"Nice to see you're making new friends."

"That's what happens when I try to be social."

Selby's weaving through the masses en-route to us. When she arrives she launches at Lloyd, open palming his chest. Upon contact, the music picks up, as do the murmurs.

"Well look who it is." She enters his armpit for a side-hug, disappearing almost entirely.

"Nice to see you Sel."

Zac approaches too and the men shake hands and tap each others biceps. Zac seems impressed by the size of him and Lloyd is kind enough to return the compliment even though to liken Zac to a stringbean wouldn't be mean at all. Selby's got her hand around my wrist again, now she's leading me through the kitchen, passed slamming shot glasses and drunken congregations toward the unpopulated corner of the balcony by the derelict table for two. She positions herself so she has her back to her co-stars who adorn the fire escape.

"Lou, can you please help me with something? Totally cool if it's not feasible."

Her tone is muted and I'm intrigued by the secrecy.

"What is it?"

Zac's making his way outside, followed by Lloyd. The co-stars gape at the sight of him like they're waiting for him to say a catchphrase or something.

"So here's the thing," Selby continues. "HP got a weird call from Alexis and it turns out he's not going to make it tonight—some logistical dilemma. He seems confident though—HP, that is—because Aaron, you know little Aaron? He's gonna play Prometheus."

"Aaron's gonna play Prometheus?" Zac echoes as he approaches. "But he's half his size."

"It's irrelevant." Selby hisses. The message like sword through his gut. His face contracts from the strike and he notices me noticing. Selby frowns but not at him and I relate with a pain in my chest.

"The problem is, HP got this half confirmation from him—Aaron, that is— and now he's not answering his phone and it's curtains in three hours. It's going to be a shit-show anyway, so well done for Harris for booking a midnight session, but how would you feel about going to run lines with him—slash—confirm he's coming? I would do it, but I need to make some serious Prometheus costume revisions and I'd ask one of these guys, but he thinks it'll throw 'em off. Said he's gonna tell them before curtains and hope for the best."

In her hands is a rolled up document, presumably the script. It's a much thinner version than the original.

"A few run-throughs to buffer his confidence a little. HP has narrowed it down."

"It wouldn't be a problem," I tell her, "but I don't have my bike and buses only run—"

"You can borrow mine," she insists.

I look to Lloyd for back-up and he's looking back at me, telling me how much everything has changed.

"I'd be down for a commute," he weighs in then looks to Zac. "Can I borrow your bike?"

Zac shrugs and takes a swig from his beer while Selby's waiting for me to nod. When I do, she relaxes and smiles warmly, then hugs me and tells me her lock combo, then she goes inside and Zac sits on the table, finishing is beer in one breath and Lloyd squeezes his shoulder, looking concerned. DJ Simon arrives then, so I begin my descent.

When we're on the last turn of the fire escape, Lloyd points his bottle in the direction of The Dope Haus.

"That's pretty sweet."

"What? Their fort?"

"The wall."

"Ah," The graffiti. "They did that soon after you left. The one night I'm not watching they do it."

"It would've been Tex."

"Which one is Tex? Severe eyebrows?"

"He's about five-nine and wears a hearing aid."

I hold an inch of space between my thumb and index finger and position his face between it. Lights from the alleyway illuminate his hair, shadowing the circles under his eyes. "They all look about this big from up here," I tell him.

He takes the lead to open the gate, leaving his bottle on the gravel road by the fence while I turn the combination to read 8-1-1-0. Lloyd lifts Zac's bike off the hook with ease.

"Have you seen those birds around town with the speech bubbles?" he asks.

"Quiet? Careful? Take it to the limit?"

"Yeah? So?"

He lifts his eyebrows in the direction of The Dope Haus.

"Did he do those?"

"We both did. In third year."

"*You* did?"

"Well, I stood guard."

"I didn't know you knew him."

"We're aquainted," he shrugs. "Different priorities."

"So what's the verdict on the latest?"

"You mean writing 'The Dope Haus' on the wall of his backyard?"

"Yeah."

"It's just like him."

"Well, I like it. I like those birds too."

"He's a good guy, Tex. Super smart. Doing his PhD over at Uscray."

"You're kidding?"

Lloyd looks confused. "What?"

I'm considering telling him about the recent developments, the interconnectedness, but I can't really find the brain power to separate the thoughts into words, and then this hologram plays out between us; it's a birds-eye view of that night in Rachel's office, the part where Dynamite says, *isn't it exhausting, asking all these questions?* So I mount Selby's bike, and start pedalling as fast as I can.

THE LIMIT

Apparently there's a bike path two underpasses north which can take a cyclist to Uscray in about a third of the mainstream commute and with twenty percent less effort. This time of night it's also host to a pretty spectacular firefly show. Lloyd's up ahead, shirt billowing in the breeze while beads of light hover around him like they know his celebrity. A hefty breeze blasts my face, which I'm grateful for, and I feel especially grateful we've got separate modes of transport and a considered distance between us.

After we pass the playground with the swing too small for my pelvis, we turn off onto a sidestreet and Lloyd slows so he's riding next to me. Naturally, I speed up, but half a block later he calls my name because he's stopped, waiting in the middle of the street. He looks like an advertisement for Zac's bike which looks so fragile beneath him, like a weak little paper clip. He's looking upward to a rooftop, smile lines deepening on the left side of his face. As I arrive on his left side, I notice one of Tex's birds, dulled in colour from the lack of pigments available.

TAKE IT TO THE LIMIT.

"We did that one before my first senior game."

"And did you take it? To the limit? One more time?"

He laughs a laugh from his nose. "Well, Lou Lou, it just so happens that the limit is illusory. As you close in, you just expect more from yourself or people expect more from you. Therein lies the problem."

With one swift manoeuvre he removes the bike from underneath him so it's on his right side. "How urgent is this mission Lou? Can we walk for a bit?"

"Well, this script is much thinner than the last one, but we should probably advance at a considered pace."

Walking brings about a calmness, a quiet. The only sounds come from cars sweeping by streets away and the rustling of leaves when the wind blows. I'm searching for something to say but all there is is me searching for something to say. With every step, he seems to get taller, more solid, more real. His jawbone moves like he's chewing his words. Soon enough he notices me noticing and when he looks down at me, his chest inflates.

"Are you gonna keep looking at me or are you gonna tell me what's going on?"

"Nothing's going on," I tell him. He raises his eyebrows and I sigh. "It's been a weird week. I did a lot of activities."

"What kind of activities?"

"Nothing of consequence."

He gives me a look asking me to cut the crap so I consider his question in the shine of the bitumen.

"Okay, let's see...how can summize this? As you know I left school, and I'm employed no more, so until recently I've been biking around, sitting in parks, wind tunnels, etcetera. That was until some hooligan stole my bike, so now I take long walks instead. For cashflow I subject myself to medical experiments, oh, and lately I've been loitering at a retirement village to frequent a friend of mine. He's an ancient man and the most articulate guy I know. "

I summon the courage to guage his expression and verify I'm not joking, but he's already aware of it and doesn't seem to find any of it very unusual.

"Yes, I hear myself."

"And are you happy?"

Am I happy?

"No, not at all."

"Why not?"

Because you're not here.

Because I'm aimless and I used to be sure.

Because I can't explain myself.

He rubs his temple with the tips of his fingers and breathes out his nose, offering a smile of sorts like he heard all of that.

"The house is in jeopardy Lou. I have to sell it."

"What? When?"

"It's underway—end of the month. This all happened this week. The last two days, in fact. I'm really sorry."

A car sweeps by at the cross street ahead, taking with it the remnants of the foundations I used to know.

"Don't be sorry," I tell him. "It's probably a good thing. Too many people know where I live."

"But what are you going to do?"

"Probably spend some time wallowing then find a contingency plan."

He pushes me like an uncle would push his nine-year-old nephew.

"You're all right Lou. I know sometimes it seems like you're not doing any-thing, but you are."

I figure a *no, I'm really not* would dull the colour of him and it really was too nice a sight; the streetlight glowing, his face right there. When I look at his face, the air flows in without much effort— at least a quarter cup. He tips his head back to the sky, looking like a superhero on holiday.

"So, apart from the huge decrease in your physique, is it everything you dreamed it would be?"

I regret the question immediately because his head dips and he sighs out heavy. He clenches the handlebars tighter and swallows.

"I'm out of the game Lou."

"What do you mean you're *out of the game*?"

"You want the short version or the long version?"

"What do you think?"

Now he's the one looking for answers in the shine of the bitumen. A car enters the street behind us and he ushers me over to the curb. When it turns at the upcoming t-section, he speaks again.

"It wasn't it."

"It wasn't what you imagined?"

"Well, that's the thing—I don't even think I even imagined it. Not that part, not really."

He swallows again and we veer back to the middle of the road.

"Mostly I coasted on what Dad said, what Coach was telling me. Always aiming for this end goal, but there is no end goal, it keeps going and I didn't like it. They don't tell you. They tell you as much as they want you to know."

His voice has the pace of a resolved man with some pent up rage. Muscles on his forearm move like slippery pebbles as he grips the handlebars.

"Being so concentrated on one thing all the time—it's mental. It's a mental game and I don't mean in the way of strategy. We don't feel our way to the perfect play—it's all plots and predictions and repeat, so much repeat. "

He looks at me sideways and purses his lips, contemplating.

"This'll sound weird but it's like I was the ball in a pinball machine, going here, going there, bouncing off him and them, and that. This procedure and that re-gime, but since Dad passed, with that huge, prevalent voice out of play, everything felt so... small, you know?"

Yes. I do know.

"It became so clear, like this veil dropped. They'll tell us exactly what we need to hear but only when we're close to breaking point, it's brutal Lou, and I could see it in the other guys too, you retain eye-contact for that extra second where they feel it and I see it but they haven't said anything so I don't say anything and it's all the same if we dont say anything, so that's what we do, and so it goes on." His elbow grazes my upper arm. "I have a feeling you're in a similar boat?"

A laugh falls out my nose because my throats ceases up at the prospect of talking about it. He prods me again, for answers this time and it takes the length of two houses to string the words together.

"I keep waiting... for this finger to come out of the sky, pointing between my eyes, telling me I'm doing it all wrong."

He smiles so his eyes are cresent moons and it makes me want to cry. I soften and I'm so grateful I have the bike supporting me.

"Has it happened yet?"

"I don't know. Is it behind me?"

He looks over his shoulder and shakes his head.

"Just road."

We take a wide berth around the corner to a side street with a lower street light ratio and this wafting sensation circulates, like an internal breeze, carrying his words about mental games.

"Maybe you oughta talk to someone?" he broaches softly. "I spoke to a counselor and she really put things into perspective for me. It can be really hard to see outside of yourself sometimes."

"I talk to plenty of people and they're all telling me exactly what I need to hear, but it's like the hardware isn't quite ready for the new software yet."

Lloyd nods the smallest of nods like he knows what I mean.

"Things are moving though," I tell him, my voice unsteady because of this lump developing in my airways. I clear my throat. "My thumbs feel a lot better since I rode into the back of a van."

I sneak a glance and his expression is equal parts surprised, curious and amused, but doesn't press for clarification. Neither of us says anything for the length of three houses.

"Lloyd?"

He looks down instead of asking *what?*

"What do you know of the amygdala?"

"The what?"

"Tex spoke about it once, this place in your brain."

"Not a whole lot, sorry Lou."

"He said you can make magic from there. I imagine it like this projector, like in a cinema, and it creates all this." I wipe my hand over the street scene hoping some shimmering effect might occur to emphasise my point. It doesn't, and I'm disappointed. "How about this one—why are my shoulders so tight since I started riding my bike?"

"Attention misplacement," he responds instantly. "That's the short version, do you want the long version?"

I look at him.

"Well for me, I find that most of the time the muscle I'm trying to work isn't even getting it, because I'm squeezing so tight that my palms burn raw, or my knees are locked so I'm using more of my lats. See, it's never really the place you're working. I mean it is, but there's more to it than that."

He looks arounds for a better explaination.

"That initial tension, what you feel in your shoulders—it's like an alert saying *go here*. So I go see what it is and once I'm there and look around, I realise it's not there at all, and I'm directed to my hips. So I look there and realise I've got all this tension there too, because I'm leaning forward too much, so my chest is shut down, so no wonder my hips are so tight. So I adjust my posture and the tops of my feet become apparent, my ankles too, and ten places later I realize I don't really trust the ground underneath me is supporting me, so there's no solidity to my foundation. It really has nothing to do with the weight on the bar. Does that make sense?"

"So much sense."

"So I guess the more I follow the sensation and explore then tension, I notice it's not real, but it's directing me elsewhere, so I look at the other possible avenues instead of straining this one place that I *think* needs the work, and more often than not, I can find the right avenue which leads to that slight shift that's going to make everything else work so much better than before. It's as much in the front as it's in the back. As much muscular as it is skeletal. As much circulatory as it is vestibular. Just as much out as in. And you know what is nuts?"

Me?

"With concentrated isolation, the work is so much easier, no stress and for less time. I'm working just four hours a week now Lou. Used to be that per day."

I've stopped in the middle of the road because we've walked way passed the Caledonian, but I can't bring myself to call his name because of this lump in my throat... expanding. The top of my mouth to opens up so my brain is spacious, and I notice this marble in the centre of my chest, solid behind my spine—or in front of it—I can't really tell. I'm searching around it, looking for an avenue to access it so I can shift it, but it's stuck. In fact, it's swelling up.

He's continuing ahead pushing that feeble-looking bike. After about ten me-tres, he notices I've stopped and stops too so we're standing there looking at each other with these bikes at our sides. I point to the building and he invites me to lead the way. Each crunch of the gravel path enlarges the marble even more.

"You know Lou, it'd probably help if you let your heels touch the ground when you walk. Can't be good for you getting around on your toes all the time."

UP-ENDED

I don't know if it's the bright lights or the white walls or the chlorine smell or his smell but my head takes on the qualities of a hot air balloon; filled with this lightness, but burning heat along this one neural pathway leading straight to the marble, which is now the size of an 8-ball turning in a slow rotation.

After three rounds of knocking, the door opens and Aaron's behind it with this spaced-out look on his face like he's taken on the role of Prometheus already — all stoic and void. He looks between me and Lloyd, then turns to walk down the hall without saying a word. I follow him down the hall. He's wearing yellow dish-washing gloves.

"Are you ready for your stage debut?" I ask.

He doesn't answer. Instead, he picks up the vacuum cleaner and turns it on with his socked foot and starts vaccuming vigourously.

The entire apartment has been up-ended; chairs on the kitchen table, random sections of books are stacked on the floor. One of the couches is now sideways so they're in a Z-formation and rags are dotted around the place. Lloyd looks perplexed. I don't know Aaron well enough to know if this is normal behaviour. Eventually he drops the vacuum and presses the off button, so I repeat my previous question.

"I am," he tells me, spraying the coffee table with furniture polish. It fizzes and expands, and when he wipes through it with haste the TV remote goes flying toward the TV, hitting the border and bouncing once the floor. He continues wiping, then sprays again.

"I'm only a size eight. He's a thirteen and I'm an eight."

Aaron's face is condensed like he's trying to prevent a fly from getting up his nose. He's shaking his head in quick, small shakes. He looks at me like he's about to cry.

"I think I breathed in too many toxic fumes. Is that a thing?"

"Yes, it's a thing."

I lead him to the couch. He's malleable in his motions, lightweight like he's vacuumed out all his energy and all his bones.

"Here, sit."

He sits on the edge of the couch and cups both hands over his knee caps. Lloyd sits on the ajoining couch so all our knees are within a one-metre diametre. The fly tries to get in again. Aaron shakes his head fervently.

"I feel weird. It's like I can see the back corner of my brain going left."

"Take a deep breath." I tell him. His eyes go wide but he doesn't take in any air.

"Too many warnings. Too many warnings and they all caught up with him. Both of them. Now I'm here all by myself and it's so quiet."

"Too many warnings about what?"

"Lex's in jail. D too."

What?

"In jail? Why?"

Aaron's X folds with concern.

"They made worse decisions a higher priority."

Because of the magic trick?

The living room is silent, but at the same time it's like the vacuum is still on. Their absence is palpable. The kitchen holds no life. The cereal cupboard unattended. Aaron's blinking excessively like the fly's trying a different route. Saliva bubbles behind my ears with no where to go.

"You're Big Lloyd Sumner, aren't you? I really hope you are."

"Yeah man. That's me."

"Alexis is my cousin. He wears your number, but he says it's because of Montagne though, not you."

"That's fair. Montagne is in great form."

Aaron falls out of his rigid position, slumping into the couch, bringing his knees to his chest and scanning the space between them.

"He must be so scared. Wouldn't you be scared? I mean, he's a big guy— Lex. I guess D is too. He's tall, but not as big as Lex. Do you think they know about D's books? Do you think that'll make a difference if we show them?"

Aaron looks to Lloyd for answers, then notices the script rolled up in his hands.

"What's that you've got there? Another script for Lex? I don't know how we'll get it to him. He did say visiting hours are ten 'til three but I'll have to double check. There's a message on the answering machine. Couldn't hear it very well though. "

"This is the script man, for you." Lloyd says gently. "It's for the play, which is tonight. You've been recommended to play Prometheus, but only if you feel up for it?"

Aaron's looking between Lloyd and the script, trying to make sense of what he said. Lloyd extends it towards him and after a moment, Aaron takes it.

"Oh—it's PMP." His eyes de-glaze as he flicks through the pages. Some sections are highlighted pink, passages no more than two lines at a time.

"I knew about that. It's tonight. It's soon." Aaron says, flicking pages. "I think he knew. I think he knew and he's been prepping me. He's been telling me all about Prometheus and how he's a warrior born on the Equinox so he's got this champion spirit that divides the worlds so the good parts last. I'm not sure I really get it, but it's only two scenes of talking, the rest is battle scenes with a sword made of al-foil. We rehearsed that part a lot."

The pages of the script fan to a close and Aaron seems lighter, like the pages, and the memory, have grounded him somehow.

"He's been prepping me. I think he knew."

"That sounds pretty cool," Lloyd says. "Maybe stepping into another world tonight wouldn't be so bad?"

Aaron looks over to me like he's only just realised I'm there, then he looks to Lloyd.

"Louise said you're smaller than TV makes you out to be, which is a bit true. You're about the same size as Alexis."

Lloyd looks at me, amusement in his expression.

"Oh yeah? What else did she say."

"She said she didn't really know you and you make good lasagne."

"Part of that is true."

"Are the trade rumours true? Are you really leaving us?"

"Something is certainly changing next season, but nothing's set in stone yet."

"I heard your girlfriend is pregnant. That's good news."

Lloyd looks at me.

All the air leaves the room. Not a single dose remains.

Aaron falls away, the roof falls away,

the floor's gone and I'm floating.

No couch beneath me.

Pressure on my ear. I'm underwater. I'm still underwater. Blessed-be.

"Hey man, do you have that sword here?"

"I do. I'll go get it."

Aaron's off the couch so I bounce up a few inches. The motion: *momentous*. So much so I've launched. I've launched and I'm in space—suspended. Orbiting.

"Lou?"

"I can see you're internalizing something. What is it?"

I have no words.

Amina floats by. *Who's it gonna help?*

Rachel emerges. She's reading a book entitled 'Distorted Shape'.

"Lou?"

"I'm thinking about steriods."

My words. Disconnected words.

He laughs. "Why?"

I just look at him. I drink his prescence in.

.

"Holy shit."

"Yeah, I know."

A whistle blows.

Aaron's moving in my periphery.

Is he nodding?

Waiting?

Involved?

I can't tell. The room has transformed into something of an impressionist painting.

After a moment his outline refines and he's aiming the sword right between my eyes. It's about the size of him plus a half and looks authentic from my angle.

"Maybe it'll be good for him, don't you think Louise?" Aaron's moving the sword in a figure eight motion. "He's always been worried about the past catching up with him—it's like he bought it on himself. Maybe it's good that he's facing it. A clean slate, you know? He can finally move on from it once and for all. "

He glistens.

If you think so.

"Oh, I forgot to tell you." He slices the sword through the air to the other side of the room.

"5D asked her."

His words echo a few times before I catch on.

5D.

"Double-D? Did she say yes?"

"No."

"She said no?"

"No, she said, *do you really want to be married?*"

Oh.

"And what'd he say?"

"He didn't say anything."

"So what happened?"

"I don't know. I guess they went inside."

Through the blur, I notice Lloyd squeezing his palms together like he's wringing out a sponge. Aaron centres the sword in front of his body in a ceremonial fashion.

"A prayer for the night" he announces and closes his eyes.

Lloyd and I exhange a look and Aaron clears his throat, so I close my eyes too, grateful for the escape, however marginal.

"Alexis—he has a clean slate. No more fear of the past. No more shadows No more fucking home phone. He's free and he's happy and he's got a nice girl on his arm."

Lloyd shifts in his seat. The 8-ball expands.

"Jarrad—he's in his element. Dope material at his fingertips *and* an abundance of time without distractions. No more struggling against the system."

Please let this kid's mourning process influence mine.

"And tonight—we all go into another realm and make the good parts last."

It's silent for a long stretch so I open one eye. Aaron's remain closed like he's still enjoying the visuals and Lloyd's aren't closed at all—quite the opposite in fact. I swallow heavy and inertia feels much slower in hindsight, like I've not quite landed yet.

Just notice.

With a breath, I do my best to suffuse the solidity of the 8-ball, hoping for some measure to my tone.

"I can't imagine a person better suited to bench press a little one," I tell him. His eyes soften, his jaw relaxes and an exhale escapes his lips. Aaron's looking between us with one eye open.

"So, what happens in the second act?" I ask him.

His smile opens the other eye and his X moves up and inch.

"You really wanna know?"

"Yes." I tell him.

Tell me every possible detail.

TRANSLUSCENT

I'm on the twenty-fourth step and I'm unprepared to face the disorder of a post-party, pre-eviction home, so I settle in the neighbours deck chair and press my feet against the cool black railing between me and the park. Inside the house, floorboards buckle and the vacuum finds the occasional bottle-cap.

Jojo's rolling side to side like she's trying to scratch an itch or get dirty or clean or something, and her owner looks tired, like he arrived at the party just after I left and has only made his way down now. He seems happy though, to be where he is. Occasionally the treetops move and more sky shows, and when that happens remnants of the evening play back like I still need a few more replays before I can figure out where to go from here.

The birds sound like birds, accenting industry with lightness and Gustave's by my side resting in a shadow. When the vacuum buzz alleviates, he runs away and Zac appears in the doorway with this purple blob morphing over his head. Blue teeth shine inverse against the brickwork and through the colours, a glass of water emerges, extended in my direction. I take it from him while the rest of his details come into view. He's got a book under his armpit and evidence of the night around his eyes. Moving slowly, he lowers his body to the top step, spreads his legs over the next four, then opens the book to a page where his thumb is.

"Listen to this," he clears husk from his throat and finds the spot he's looking for. "The pair approached work in a remarkably lackadaisical manner. Their days were made up of several hours of tennis, copious amounts of tea and they often lost interest in the project altogether. The most significant revelations came during chance conversations on their morning walks where their minds spun around the problem until they broke the code."

He closes the book and gives me a sideways glance, then looks out to the park as the book hangs between his knees.

"I like that. Who are *they*?"

"The guys who discovered the Laws of Electromagnetism. It's like what you're doing—not the physics part obviously, but still, the lackadaisical bit."

He catches me profiling him and turns to face me.

"What are you doing today?"

"I'm going to jail later then I have a meeting."

"Do you have time to help me with something?"

"Yeah, what is it?"

"I got these walkie talkies and I wanna see what kind of range they get."

"I can do that."

He stands on the top step so he's about twice as tall as me from this angle.

"Wait there."

"I can do that too."

He goes inside and the floorboards creak accordingly. Overhead, a plane scans through the blue sections of sky and some weird little bugs in the grass sound like they're playing with slinkies. A car drives by below, crunching over gravel and Zac soon returns, holding out the device with a red light in the corner indicating 'on' mode. I press the button and radio static sounds.

"I'll start walking," he says into the talkie. "And we'll keep in contact like this—over."

"Got it," I say into mine.

"Then say—over."

"Do we have to do over? We normally don't say more than three words to each other as it is."

"Yeah, you're right. Ok, forgo over."

- Now?

- Yeah.

- Now?

- Yeah.

- Now?

- Yeah, but with slight crackles.

- I'm gonna run a bit.

- Now?

- Yeah. No crackles.

- How bout now?

- Yeah. What do you see?

- What do I see?

- Yeah, what's happening over there? I can't see you anymore.

- Um... there's an archery squad. Four members. Two girls and two dads.

- What else?

- A girl on the other side of the road is lifting her knees real high like she's preparing to run with her knees real high.

He doesn't hear my laugh because I don't press the button.

- What else?

- I can hear Celine Dion playing from a window.

- I don't understand why people don't like Celine.

- They do at home. Or when they're sick in hospital and have nothing to lose.

- What else?

- Kids playing. A dad is having a picnic with his little baby daughter. He's looking right at her. She's watching bee's fly.

Zac comes back into view, the side of him anyway. Enough of him that I can see the back of his ear glow pink and translucent. He's leaning on a tree by the rotunda with the walkie-talkie at his mouth, then by his side, then at his mouth, then by his side again. Static sounds twice, then silence as he slides down the trunk to sit on the roots. His head drops so he's looking at the dirt while the walkie-talkie hangs loose in his hand.

- I have a theory.

His head goes up and so does the walkie-talkie.

- What is it?

- Good, bad. The best, the worst. I love, I hate. We can't conclude anything—ever.

- That's Parchment's theory.

- You're an extremist either way.

- Apparently.

- Do you think he's right?

- Who's to say?

Zac can't see it from where he's facing, but Selby's entering the other side of the park with the knee-high runner in hot pursuit.

- We've got a confirmed sighting of Selby due east.

Static again as the runner drops Selby's tail and takes the corner down Birchmore.

- Is she leaving me?   Over.

EQUANIMITY

Alexis greets me with a smile out of place in this context which tells me he's either still coming to terms with his new reality, or, he's content with the idea of facing his past. It could also be that he's a much better actor than he gives himself credit for. Either way, he's much too bright for the surroundings. Too alive to be contained.

He pulls out the chair opposite and the legs screech against the lino which irks the guy at the next table over who looks like a version of Neil who can't swim, took too many wrong turns and didn't have his own Norma. Alexis doesn't let it touch him. He hitches up his rolled-up sleeves.

"Aaron told me the visiting hours." I tell him.

"The kid's got a beautiful vision but a poor filtration system."

"I like his vision, and his filtration system. And I hate to lay more bad news on you, but he makes a pretty good Prometheus too. I don't think you'll be cast next season."

He laughs out loud much to our neighbour's dismay. It's a lovely sound.

"My tights would've come up to his neck."

"Selby's fit real nice."

Three guards monitor the room, watching their quadrants for slights of hands and suspicious behaviour. They exhibit many years of worry and concern in their features. One of them steps in to separate a couple who kiss fast and furiously over their table.

"Is Dynamite in here with you?"

"Yeah." Alexis looks into the tabletop, squeezing tiny invisible handlebars.

"Does he get to draw?"

"They give us a stack of paper and crayons when we're good."

I can't tell if he's joking but it's the answer I want to hear so I don't ask if he's serious. Instead, I search for the story I'd memorized on the bus ride over which seems to have been erased about the time I walked through the x-ray scanner.

Alexis's looking at me quizzically, scanning my hairline, the frizz and the sweat.

"What? My hair is ridiculous isn't it? Who cuts your hair? Is he around?"

"Aren't you going to ask me what I did to end up in this whack suit?"

"I know what you did," I tell him. "You did a magic trick with the wrong people who didn't believe in you. Happens all the time."

Alexis's chest expands and his hands go under the table. Today he's wearing a lot more numbers than thirteen.

"What's it like in here?"

"It's not good Lou, but it's not bad. Could be worse."

He sighs across the table and looks over his shoulder.

"You know my bike got stolen after all," I tell him.

"I warned you about that. There's a bunch of no-gooders on campus."

He gestures to himself, so aware, and yet still unable to grasp what it means to permanently mark a declaration of love for his family on his face.

"Can I do a thing?"

"You can do whatever you want—you're not locked up."

"Does the girl know you're here?"

His circumference deflates, cheekbones get rigid and suddenly he's small in his chair, completely bottomed-out.

"It might be the perfect time to see if she likes you for who you really are."

"This isn't who I am, it's something I did once. Well—three times."

"That's what I mean though—remove the conditions; just you, stripped down bare against the walls. Metaphorically, of course."

"It's not a good look, Louisa, look at me."

"Honestly, I really don't think she'll care."

"Imagine the torture though, I wouldn't be able to do anything."

It goes left eye, right eye, left eye, right. Eyes glistening *thank you*. Chest spread like *thank you*. All he's saying is *thank you*. The prisoner emanating gratitude, although, he really isn't a prisoner at all. He's got the same look about him as Neil at six o'clock on a Monday morning.

A buzzer sounds indicating our time is up which seems invasively premature. We scrape our chairs along the floor, and even though he knows it's going to cause him grief, he hugs me *thank you* then squeezes my shoulders.

"Shame about your bike."

"Isn't it just."

HALLUCINATION

Rachel looks calm like I haven't abused her trust at all. She's sorting through a stack of folders, none of them manila. The floor's covered in boxes and most of the shelves have been cleared. Her accolades are off the wall and it smells like cardboard and air freshener.

"Have a seat Louise. I'll be one second."

I sit and listen to the seconds pass, sounding more like a countdown than a passing measure. The window sill is plantless. Dark grey clouds journey by.

"Are you relocating?" I ask her.

"In a sense." She puts the lid on a box and makes her way to her chair. "Okay, where're we at?"

"I'm not sure, but there's something I need to tell you."

She leans back, eyes widening slighty ready for the information. I can't quite tell if she's being passive aggressive about recent events or if she's above all that transpired and doesn't care at all. I intake half a cup, as much as my handlebar shoulders will allow.

"There may have been some fallacies on the initial questionnaire we filled out on my first day, and when I say may have been, I mean there definitely are some."

She pauses me with one finger and looks around the office, landing her gaze on a pile of boxes by the door, then she heads over to them and from the top one she retrieves the PSOH folder. On her way back to the desk she flicks through the pages and extracts a questionnaire, presumably mine.

"Okay, go ahead," she invites.

"I have smoked pot in the last six months, or at least, that would've been true when the study started."

She simply gazes at me over the top of her glasses.

"Ok great, thanks for telling me. Anything else?"

"Does that matter?"

"About the pot?"

"Yeah."

"Why are you asking if it matters?"

"Because it matters to some people in these situations."

"Does it matter to you?"

Uh—what? Does it matter to me?

"I thought it might affect your data."

She smiles, her eyes pressing into mine like she's waiting for me to get it.

Get what?

Does it matter to me?

Oh.

I see.

"Good point."

"Actually Louise, I have something I have to tell you too. We've come to the end of the study."

I motion to the bare walls. "Yes, I can see that."

"Well, yes, there's that, but also, the study is complete. There is no third part. No interview."

"I'm not following..."

"The study, Louise, was looking at follow-through in relation to monetary re-ward. The level of discomfort one will endure for altruistic purposes. You might've noticed the first load of compensation you received outside that day was almost the whole amount, even though there was still another cognition test and an interview, supposedly."

"So what? You didn't expect me to come back?"

"Well, therein lies the question. There was no expectation. Whatever happened, happened."

With that, Rachel spins ninety degrees toward the filing cabinet and retrieves an envelope from the top. She offers it to me but I don't move to take it.

"It's okay to take it Louise. You've earned it."

I take the envelope, feeling the weight of an ending in its contents.

"Why those words?"

"What words?"

"Hid and head."

"They're just the ones that came to me."

Right.

"So what's your hypothesis feeding into?"

Rachel levels her gaze and seems to settle in her chair.

"That, Louise, is a perfect question and something I can't answer. Remem-berwhen we first met I told you that the aim of the study has morphed? Well, this whole thing is teetering on vague—again."

"So you're giving up?" I sound accusatory. I'm projecting and it's at this moment it feels like she knows more about me than the information I provided that first day. Off come her glasses, which she folds and puts on the desk in front of her. Then she clasps her hands and leans in.

"No, I'm not giving up. Not everything is that straightforward. Not in research, not in life. You can't force results. Any time you try to force anything you're moving away from your goal. We're taught to move from a place of effort, from hard work, from a place of haste and I've spent my career filling up my days, moving from one hypothesis to the next, testing out all these variables to see what happens only to restart from some other angle."

"But it all matters doesn't it? It all feeds into the next?"

Her mouth curves into a smile.

"Of course. Like everything."

She goes on to tell me something silently then, I feel like it's about Owen, but I can't quite tell.

"But doesn't it feel like a waste?"

She shakes her head.

"Space and time are required to reconcile the data and set a new course. I think you might know a bit about that."

Holy fuck.

"You know Louise, I think everyone has their own version of your handlebar shoulders. It's worth exploring, but it's important not to place too much emphasis on one particular symptom though, there's always more to it than that. I think that's key." She presses her palm just above her right breast. "I feel mine most when I leave my daughter. This pain, a swelling—right here. It's my whole lymphatic system though. I'm too rigid, always have been. Not enough flow."

She laughs one laugh from her nose.

"She escaped that day you saw Tanya for the second test. Sweet little thing, one year old and fleeing my mother's custody."

"She escaped?"

Rachel nods. "Embarked on a solo mission down the street to find me. I lost my shit, obviously, but it was a blessing really, it made me realise that this work, my work, the underlying pretence of all of it is fear—like you heard in my lecture.

I always thought if I delved into it, if I studied it in others, I'd be able to understand it in myself more. And I did, and layers came off, many layers, but it never really ends, you know? There's always more to learn, more to discover, and I don't think we'd ever want there not to because then there's no growth. So why work now if the vision isn't clear. It's movement for movements sake. It's like trying to fill a bucket with a hole in the bottom. It doesn't fulfill me, it drains me. It takes me away from what feels good and now I know what makes me feel good. She makes me feel good, so that's where I'll go."

"Attention misplacement." Lloyd's words leave me so instinctively my head floats back from the output.

"Exactly."

It goes left eye, right eye, left eye, right eye and I have nothing else to say. The pulse of my heartbeat becomes me. I feel it in head, behind my eyes, in my shoulders.

"So thank you for participating and thanks for coming back. I understand you might feel a little disjointed by the deception, so we can go through a debrief which goes into a deeper explanation of—"

"No, that's fine."

"Are you sure?"

"So sure."

She smiles warmly, a smile goodbye.

"It's a bit bullshit, isn't it? All that repetition?"

I couldn't agree more.

"Rachel, about the initial questionnaire..."

"Another one?"

"The question asking whether I suffer from hallucinations, you can change my *no* to a *yes*—it seems my whole life has been one."

—◇—

Just as I'm about to jump down the last three steps, Mary's non-friends appear through the double doors. They make a special effort to press themselves against the wall to avoid close contact with me which I celebrate internally and thank them for emphatically.

With one push of the railing I'm ejected into the quad where it's belting down rain. The whole scene is dark like I've been sitting in Rachel's office for half the day or more. Orange orbs glow, slick black shapes run for cover and a bright yellow raincoat is reversing a bike—*my bike*—into the bike rack, exactly where I left it. From the hood of the raincoat, a trail of red hair peeks out.

APOGEE

No fireflies yet, it's too early for that. Gravel shoots out behind me sending mud splashing up my back. I really don't mind though; the dirt would wash out—it just felt good to be moving again.

No end goal. Only path.

The time on foot has strengthened those smaller, seemingly inconsequential muscles that Lloyd spoke of. As much in the front as the back. As much muscular as it is skeletal. As much out as in.

It's all connected.

Exertion feels minimal, like the path is moving underneath me, *for me*, and the underpasses feel effortless like the traffic is helping me up the incline. Up ahead, a pool of sunlight shines reflective over the next stretch so houses reflect inverse on the road. Petals bloom electric like they've been switched on for the first time and residual drops make their way down from treetops, aiming for my bare eyeball which meets with momentum resulting in a fantastic blur.

I'm two blocks from home hoping someone will be there to hear about the bike re-acquisition, but when I turn down our street I hit an invisible wall. My back wheel stops so I'm slipping over bitumen, then I come to a full halt, completely drunk off contrast. It takes me a long moment to understand what I'm looking at.

It's all so glossy, like a trick of the light.

Hanging over the glistening brickwork are Selby's map drawings, three of them, completely saturated and lit up gold in patches. The ink is running, the borders blurring and all the lines she'd outlined so perfectly melt into rivers of pink and purple with tendrils of green which catch and intensify in certain areas.

There wasn't anything to do—the damage had been done.

The last one nearest the vines hangs on by the corner, on the cusp of crashing below. I stand there waiting for it to happen, feeling the bitumen press up into my heels with this pain in my chest for all the lovely people.

Even though they would never be how they once were or how she might've intended, they'd transformed into something else entirely, and from where I stood, they looked even better.

FIN

ACKNOWLEDGEMENTS

A group of people have breathed life into this story, willingly or not, but absolutely nonetheless. They may recognise themselves in these pages, in certain scenes, sentences or scenarios, and my hope is when they do, they'll feel a wave of gratitude emanating from my quarters for having helped shape this story.

I've been lucky enough to know you, intimately to both of us, or at least one of us, and for that I am grateful.

www.ingramcontent.com/pod-product-compliance
Lightning Source LLC
Chambersburg PA
CBHW050926030726
47503CB00007BB/2485